ALLYSON YOUNG

EVERNIGHT PUBLISHING ®

www.evernightpublishing.com

ALLYSON YOUNG

UNDONE BY DESTINY

Blue Star Shifters, 2

Allyson Young

Copyright © 2017

Chapter One

"We need to talk." Tahl strove to keep his tone modulated, neutral, but knew he hadn't succeeded by the way her slender body stiffened. Or maybe it was merely his presence that caused Desiree to tense. She never used to react like that around him. Before, she'd brighten, and soften somehow, like what she felt was reserved only for him. Before he understood what it meant. Before he fucked up…

"Sure." Her full lips curved into a lovely, warm smile—if one didn't notice the emotion wasn't reflected in her pale, blue eyes. In fact, winter's cruel depths might be a better description for those frosty orbs. "Maybe later today. I'll be at Jett and River's."

She wasn't overt about it. Desi could have faced him down and said they had nothing to talk about, but he suspected she was fully aware it would imply she felt something for him. Tahl desperately wanted to believe she still did—and that her adept avoidance confirmed it. He hoped.

But he didn't want to talk to her at her

brother's—his Alpha's—home. He didn't want anyone around when he made his case because he feared he was going to have to push hard to get past his perfidy. And Desiree might seek an intervention. Not that Jett or any other male was going to get in his way, though in fact he'd yet to seek his Alpha's permission.

He really wanted Desi to offer her surrender before he triggered her heat, though, and he would trigger it. Of that, he had no doubt. This thing between them had simmered for a long time, still simmered, only he'd been too stupid to notice, enthralled by a nasty piece of redheaded shifter. He'd thought on it and decided Desi had convinced herself she now hated him, and it was up to him to reverse it.

"How if we talk now?"

"I'm working, Tahl. My mother asked me to help out today." She kept smiling, although the strain showed in the slight tremble at the corner of her lips and the faint creases at the corner of her eyes.

He stepped closer and was rewarded by the dilation of her pupils and the ever so slight scent of feminine arousal. *Yes.* Gesturing around the empty boutique, he said. "It looks pretty quiet."

"I'm not blowing my responsibilities off for you." Her lips set in a straight line and now he could smell her growing anxiety.

"You have to take a break, sometime."

"Tahl!" Marlene swept in from the back, pushing more air ahead of her than a petite woman should. But then Desi's mother was far more than human. Her children didn't much resemble either of their fathers, something he'd noted early on, and there was nothing of Marlene's looks represented, either. It made a person speculate about the gene pool.

"Hello, Marlene." He leaned in to press a kiss on

her cheek, the fragrance of herbs and something citrus filling his nostrils. She'd been like a second mother to him, despite her eccentricities, or perhaps because of them. Another reason he'd dismissed his feelings for Desi as being incestuous, treating her like a little sister instead. A little sister with a huge crush...

"What brings you to *Simply Dressed*? We have some lovely new lingerie if you're looking for something for one of your lady friends."

Desiree flinched and put space between them, moving an infinitesimal distance he felt acutely. She schooled her expression, but he marked her pallor. Even as he regretted the discomfort her mother had caused by her offhand comment—deliberately, he was certain—he rejoiced in the additional proof that Desi still felt something for him. "I wasn't looking for clothing, Marlene. I was hoping to have a moment with your daughter."

An appraising glance didn't fool him. Marlene knew exactly why he was there and had chosen to rip away the subterfuge and stir the pot in the process. He wondered at her agenda before setting it aside. She passed a hand over her hair. "Well, we obviously aren't busy, so off you go."

"Mom! There's so much to do."

"I'm caught up on the paperwork, dear. And I can handle a few customers, even supposing we get a stampede."

If looks could kill, Tahl wouldn't be surprised if both he and Marlene withered to the floor. He reached for Desiree's arm, but she snatched it back. Waiting for the outburst, remembering her nature, he was surprised when she painted on another smile.

"We can talk in the office."

He'd take it. Tahl followed her slender form,

watching her tight ass appreciatively as it flexed beneath the tight pencil skirt. Her long black hair was caught up in some kind of complicated swirl and clipped in place with something shiny, and his gaze lingered on the tender nape of her neck.

Taking the chair behind the desk, the heavy structure a barrier between them, she gestured to the lone seating available. He lowered himself into it, aware she was tense and trying to hide it.

Outwaiting him, something few individuals were able to do, he took a breath. "You're nearly twenty-five."

Her full lips thinned as they pressed together before she lifted a shoulder. "Happens to us all."

"I want to claim you."

Eyes widening, she stared and then shuttered her expression, but not before he thought he read not only shock and surprise but a flare of interest. Her lips parted and he studied their softness before she set her mouth again.

"Is this some kind of a … joke?"

"Baby, c'mon. You must have noticed."

"Noticed what?"

She was going to make him work for it. That was okay. He'd hurt her some time back and didn't expect her to fall at his feet. "I've been trying to get back in your good graces since I returned to the pack. Uh, to court you." Was that even a term used anymore?

A brittle smile graced her lovely face. "Is that what you've been doing?"

"When I could get your attention for thirty seconds."

He heard Marlene moving around in the shop area and the faint sounds of traffic on the street. Maybe the sound of Desi's brain ticking over as he waited for her response. His gut tightened and his wolf paced.

"What about Peyton Leaf?"

He knew she'd want to know and had formulated any number of half-truths to share, except damned if he didn't want to lie to her. Except he absolutely couldn't tell her the truth. Masking his emotions, he said, "She has nothing to do with this."

Tilting her head, she stared at him, anxiety tightening her features. "What happened?"

"I'm not talking about it." He wanted to tell her, but he and Jett had decided to keep the entire fuck up under wraps. Not to mention he'd made a promise…

Desi's eyes flared and then filled with misery before she screened them with a dip of her long lashes. "Sorry. I'm not interested in you courting—or claiming—me." She opened a drawer in the desk and pulled out her purse.

"I'm sorry I hurt you before, baby. But I'm here now and I want you." His proclamation fell between them and echoed passionately in the small space.

For an instant, her face softened icing over with anger. "I want a mate of *my* choosing."

Watching her straighten to her full height, his wolf lunged impotently against his restraint. As she cut around the desk to make her way toward the door, he said, "I'll give you some time to think."

"I don't need it. Stay away from me, Tahl."

Staying in control as she vanished from sight nearly killed him, but he'd spooked her. He'd stated his case and Desi *would* think about it. It was the way she was made. He'd known her well, despite the wall she'd erected between them, and no one changed that much. He decided to follow up this afternoon. Best he didn't give her too much time and give her cause to try and run.

Marlene chuckled as he headed out.

"Sorry?"

"So you've decided to quit dancing around and push her."

"I'm going to talk to her again, shortly. With her." And if that didn't work … well, he'd see.

A tiny snort emanated from the woman he hoped would soon be his mother-in-law. An only child, both his parents gone in a car accident when he was in his mid-teens, he couldn't imagine belonging, by pack law, to a better family than Desiree's. Even if Marlene was an enigma, and her genetic influence, in particular, would doubtless manifest in all her children—and theirs. His and Desi's. His belly clenched when he thought about the narrow escape he'd had with the Dawnfall shifters. He might be jumping through hoops where Desi was concerned, but the idea of being mated to Peyton…

"She's past listening, Tahl. Convinced herself she's over you and has moved on. She told me a few days ago she has her eye on Kris." Marlene spoke through his musings, the way she used to talk when he spent all his free time at her home. The speculation was back in her eyes, as though she was reading his mind.

Fuck that. There wasn't a male shifter in the pack who wasn't aware of Tahl's intent—and none would dare get in his way. Whatever dabbling Desi had done, it didn't signify now, just as his considerable conquests didn't matter. That was all in the past. He reined himself in on the strength of that knowledge. "I'd rather you leave this to me, Marlene."

She sobered. "Sorry. I meddle. I know I do. River and I don't have the relationship I'd hoped for because of how outspoken I get and the way I push my opinions. So I'll back off and wish you luck."

"Thanks."

Marlene shook her head. "She's running. My poor Desiree." Her eyes narrowed and concealed the flare he'd seen. "I know I promised not to meddle, but this notion of destiny makes me sick, Tahl. I wonder how you males would feel if made powerless to your hormones."

His were pretty much ruling him at the moment, though he'd readily admit to his heart being in charge where Desiree was concerned. And to think he'd written those emotions off in the past as those being for a treasured sister. He had fiercely ignored any physical pull, convincing himself that only a pervert would experience such a thing for a young female, especially one he'd seen grow up like the sibling he'd never had. He'd never reciprocated Desiree's far-from-familial interest, though had been alerted to it by none other than his Alpha. And only when he'd declared his intent to pursue Peyton Leaf of Dawnfall.

"I'll excuse myself," he told Marlene, not waiting for a reply, and not responding to her bitter comment. Shifters were a breed unto themselves and she definitely needed to back off. Desiree would no doubt head for her brother's and he figured to show up and further their chat. He might not be as fine a strategist as Kris, that fucker, but he wasn't the Alpha's lieutenant for nothing. He decided to ignore the fact that his rank and abilities seemed to crap out around the female he wanted as his mate.

"Tahl?"

Impatiently, he turned back. Marlene stared at him from the doorway, her face reflecting her worry.

"Talk to her. Ask her to agree. Say what's in your heart."

Nothing different than what he knew he should do, though he'd been careful not to say too much the first time around. Self-preservation kept him from putting all his cards on the table, and he felt ashamed, though apparently even male shifters, ass over heels, had their pride. Nodding, he went looking for the female he'd chosen. His wolf was stirring at the idea of a chase, and he reined in the animal.

Climbing into his car—his restored Camaro had been another love for years—Tahl pulled out into traffic and headed toward his Alpha's home. Desi would be seeking River's counsel, and it seemed she'd get her wish about meeting him at her brother's. Impatience in line with his wolf's pacing, his right palm itched with the need to lay it flat on the wench's backside, given her stubbornness. He squeezed tighter to the wheel. His historic sex partners liked a bit of pain with their pleasure, but despite Desi's fiery nature, he couldn't sense her interests. *Because she closed herself off to you when you announced your intention to pursue Peyton.*

All he knew was that he'd take her any way he could get her. He knew deep down she would satisfy him, as he would her. Sex was never an issue with shifters. Well, except for a few confused shifters, and he wouldn't consider Desiree confused. Wilful, determined, bright, and beautiful better described her, and he could admit he longed for the days when they sparred and teased one another. Not like the distant manner in which they now related. God, he'd missed her.

Turning onto the last mile of road, he clicked his tongue as his Alpha's home came into view. His brow furrowed when he didn't see Desi's own sports car, yet another interest they shared. If she wasn't here yet, he'd better have some kind of plan before he knocked on the door.

His Alpha's mate, River, swung open the door as he was raising his knuckles. Her nearly two-year-old little girl slouched on her mother's hip and River made a practiced grab for her son as he made for the opening.

"Andrew. Not out the front door."

Tahl scooped his godchild up—a role he shared with Desiree—and cuddled him close. "Giving your mom fits again, kiddo?"

Andrew wiggled and demanded to be set down, and Tahl obliged once the door was shut tight. The little guy could run like the wind and kept everyone on their toes.

As he dashed toward the playroom, previously the great room, River spoke. "Here to see Jett?"

He faced her, taking in the contented glow on her face and the slight swell of her belly, denoting a third child. River had always been a lovely female, but she was positively beautiful since her relationship with Jett had solidified. "Desiree on her way here?"

"She said so." River wasn't the avoidant type, but she didn't look pleased with him.

He cursed under his breath. "But she is coming."

"So she said."

"River, it's been three years. She's coming up on her twenty-fifth birthday. I've been patient while she lived it up." It fucking well killed him to see it too. There was that double standard again, the one Marlene decried. He'd sown his share of wild oats with willing females, both shifter, and human, before setting all of that aside. Hell, he and Jett—he shut that down, right the fuck now. River couldn't read minds, but it never hurt to be careful. Anyhow, no one judged either sex for getting busy, but his wolf snarled at the thought of Desi being with anyone else.

"You were gone well over one of those years." River yanked him from his introspection.

"I owed it to Alpha Leaf. Seeing as I went there with the intention of claiming his granddaughter." He wasn't inclined to explain how he'd paid off the debt of honor to anyone other than Jett, and if his Alpha had kept that to himself, he wasn't enlightening River. The issues at Dawnfall had been terrifying, and fortunately contained within that pack, in part because of him. "And I did come home to run the show for a time when you were… Well, I came home."

He wasn't above calling in a marker when it came to working this thing out with Desiree. He'd taken care of business while River recovered from a rogue shifter attack and Jett was too worried for his mate to attend to anything else.

"And both Jett and I appreciated it. I understand you had to return to Dawnfall, but it was for a long time. Did you ever think Desi may have moved on during that period? She was pretty young when she had that crush on you."

"And you don't think it endured." He couldn't hide the despair his gut relayed to his head, even as his heart and his wolf scoffed. He *knew* Desiree was still interested.

River soothed Bella with a hand down her back, as she began to fuss at being held. "Shh, little one. Go play with your brother." As Bella toddled off, River turned back to him. "It endured. But it turned into something different. There's a fine line between like and dislike. Or love and hate."

She wasn't telling him anything he didn't know. "It's her I want."

"And if she doesn't want you?"

River was his Alpha's mate, and he afforded her much the same respect as he did Jett. But her quiet question cut to the bone and he wanted to lash out. "You didn't want Jett at the beginning."

Aside from a sharp inhalation, she didn't show much of an overt response to the dig. Jett had claimed her against her will, as tradition allowed, and it made for some interesting times, initially. "I wouldn't recommend that you push your claim, Tahl. I'm nothing like Desi." *And you're nothing like Jett.*

She didn't have to say it. He was well aware of the differences between him and his Alpha. Tahl was a black and white kind of guy, though he was trying to see shades of gray when it came to Desi. As for River and Desi … the Alpha's sister didn't have a compliant bone in her body.

"Did I hear my name?" His Alpha sauntered down the stairs, hair wet, buttoning a shirt over his broad chest.

"Tahl is here to see Desi."

"But she's not here, is she?" Jett slipped an arm around River's waist and tucked her against him, one big hand splaying across her belly.

"She's on her way." River leaned her head against her mate's shoulder and Tahl could feel them communicate. Fated mates did that, or so the old tales went, and he envied their connection.

"You still haven't given up, Tahl," his Alpha said, a commiserating look softening his eyes. Eyes the same color as his sister's, though without that distant, cold look.

"On a time clock now, Jett." He didn't know how the months had slipped by, in truth. He came back home, settled in, and took notice of Desiree—who blithely *didn't* notice him. For months and months no matter what he did.

"You know how I feel about—" River bit her lip at Jett's sideways glance. "Okay, but I think Tahl should tread carefully."

Jett tugged her long, blonde hair. "You can't dismiss our customs, sweetheart. Female shifters get claimed, and for the most part, it all works out well in the end. Like it did for us, even if it was … rushed."

River blushed and muttered something about him being lucky, and Tahl decided it was time to change the subject. At least as far as he could change it without losing sight of his objective. "I'd like to have some time alone with Desiree. When she arrives. I want to follow up on a conversation I had with her this morning."

"We can make that work." Jett easily overrode his mate's faint protest. "River, best check on Andrew and Bella. They're pretty quiet. And the nanny isn't back yet."

"I'm sure I hear them playing nicely." River hustled away, an anxious expression on her pretty face.

"They're playing with building blocks, not dismantling anything or otherwise getting into trouble. And the pool's locked, though Andrew will likely be able to circumvent that obstacle any day now," Jett said, his gaze intently following his mate. He turned to face Tahl with a wry smile. "My hearing's better than hers. Now, what's your plan?"

Tahl had heard the little ones playing as well, kept their sounds within easy access despite his distraction with Desiree. Pups were a treasure, and any adult shifter watched out for them. "I don't have a plan." He didn't. He'd come home, hung around, made himself available, given her space and stayed celibate so she couldn't misconstrue his singular interest—to no avail.

It was time he told her what was in his heart. Surely she would listen to him. He'd grovel if need be. Appeal to her somehow. The only thing he couldn't share was what transpired at Dawnfall. "Get us in a room together, alone, and I'll figure it out."

"I'll do you one better." His Alpha tossed him a key. "The cabin up north is standing empty. Take my sister up there for however long it takes."

"I believe that's called kidnapping."

"For fuck's sake, Tahl. She's miserable. You're miserable. She was crazy about you and I still see it. But my sister has more pride than anyone I know and she's painted herself into a corner. You need to give her the opportunity to step out."

His wolf prickled against his skin in avid agreement. "I'm trying to be civilized about this."

"We *aren't* civilized, buddy. Not at the heart of it."

"You are. You're driving this pack into the present with an eye on the future." And he had his Alpha's back because he believed the path they were on was righteous.

"Not always when it comes to our females." Jett's tone reflected a hint of remorse. "But damned if I can figure out the correct balance between tradition and today's times."

"You've opened the council up to them." Two select females, ones with something to offer. But then the males on the council weren't there by political appointment. They'd earned their place too.

"River helped me see the necessity, the advantage of having females dictate policy. It's a work in process. But that doesn't change the fundamental basis of claiming. Shifters mate, Tahl. Don't lose sight of that, at least until we find a better way."

"She's gonna hate me." Except they were running out of time…

"Then see to it you give her a reason to get past it."

He now had his Alpha's permission to claim Desiree. It also was tradition, what shifters did. Destiny. He wanted her, loved her, so what the fuck was he waiting for?

Turning on his heel, he strode out to the Camaro, plotting an interception course.

Chapter Two

Her brother's house was only a couple of miles away, and Desi eased up on the gas. She'd been driving around, in flight, but barreling down the roadway could garner her a speeding ticket. She snorted. That was the least of her worries, though it hadn't been that long since the last one.

Damn the man. She'd been running from him that time, too. He was always turning up wherever she was, and she was terrified he'd scent her interest. Well, her wolf's interest, because the woman wasn't taking the risk. She sidestepped him, reverted to outright avoidance and managed to circumvent any alone time over the past many months, but invariably he cornered her. That left her no choice but to walk away, making it obvious she wasn't interested—to everyone, and acting like a snobby brat. And she regretted behaving in such a manner because she'd grown up and matured, she hoped. Though surely a mature female could come up with a way to dissuade a shifter. Except, this time, he'd asserted his interest—and his intent.

She shivered. Once upon a time she'd have done anything to be cornered by that particular predator. And Tahl was, indeed, a hunter. Shoving her ridiculous, historical thoughts away, she reminded herself she'd been a young, impressionable female back then and Tahl embodied everything a susceptible heart could desire.

A faint flush crawled up her throat, heating her flesh and coloring her cheeks, and she didn't dare glance at herself in the rearview, knowing she would witness the humiliation she felt. She could still remember telling River about her crush, loftily announcing her fondest— and sexual—hopes regarding Tahl. Out freaking loud.

Like it was a done deal. Then it turned out the man in question not only hadn't even noticed her that way, he'd had his eye on a redheaded troublemaker from a totally different pack. She must have been blind. Blinded by love, because while even the thought of Tahl made her want to do all sorts of unmentionable, sexual things and caused her wolf fits, unrequited lust didn't break hearts.

Something had happened with Peyton Leaf and now Tahl was settling for Desi. Except, she wasn't interested anymore. She. Was. Not.

A familiar black shape in the distance teased her vision, coming fast, her shifter eyesight superior to a human's. "Oh, shit."

She glanced in her mirrors and stomped on the brake, pulling a credible three-point turn on the fly, relying on muscle memory. She punched the button on the steering wheel. "Call River."

"Calling River on cell," the nasal, automated voice concurred.

"Desi?" The shrill laughter of children echoed in the background.

"Tahl was there."

"He left."

"Okay." Maybe he was giving up. Heading home. Good. Great. Somehow she didn't think so, although she no longer trusted her instincts.

"You're sure about it, Desi? You aren't … interested?"

Was she? The instant she'd wrestled her car into submission, moving quickly in the other direction, she regretted it. Her response was animalistic, yet her wolf wasn't even on the same page, so why on earth was she running?

But she felt committed to flee, her manner of interacting with Tahl a habit she couldn't break, especially when he'd up stirred the embers of smoldering hope today. She risked a quick exit into the only industrial section on the outskirts of Blue Star. Her tires protested with a scream and she winced. Comforted by the looming structures, she deked across a busy yard and bumped over a rail line. She scanned for Tahl's distinctive ride and told herself she was vastly relieved not to see it. Or him.

The spurious release of adrenaline hollowed her belly and she chose a route to get her back onto the interstate. She wasn't sure where she was going, but that talk had turned her inside out. He apparently wanted her—now—and she wasn't interested. She couldn't be.

"Are you there? Desi?" The connection crackled. Probably all the surrounding metal.

"Sorry, just taking a detour."

"You're running out of time." River sounded both worried and anxious. "Have you thought about what will happen?"

How could she tell her friend that very event starred front and center in her daydreams *and* her nightmares? She'd had something quite different all planned out well over three years ago, hell since she and her wolf melded and set sights on Tahl—and now she had no idea what to do. None. While she'd been making plans, life had rolled on without her.

"I'll find myself surrounded by shifter males and one will claim me." She hadn't said it out loud before, and to hear it spoken so baldly made her want to scream in frustration. She wasn't ready. She'd never be ready. *Because the only male you want is the one you've decided you can't give the time of day.* "Unless I take a vacation and hide out someplace, wait it out until the next month. Buy myself more time."

"I planned something like that and was thwarted,

so I feel for you."

"I know, River. And you had good cause."

"No, I was confused and misled. I'll never regret being Jett's mate."

"Well, I'll be somebody's mate." *Just not Tahl's.*

"It probably won't be so bad."

"Well, you did luck out..."

River sighed audibly. "Exactly. And if you look around, most all couples have good, solid relationships."

"Sure." She should be so lucky. And less conflicted. The only man she'd wanted had looked elsewhere, and then came home, tail between his legs. Well, not exactly. But he'd returned, unmated, nearly two long years after declaring his intent to claim another, and nobody knew why. Oh, her brother would know, but despite the rampant speculation, and idle gossip, she had no clue. Not that she'd wondered. Much. Whenever anyone hinted, that gorgeous face had tightened and the inquisitor had backed the fuck off. The way she'd done earlier, maybe because she'd been afraid he'd read her guilt. *You had nothing to do with it. Quit thinking that way.*

"What are you doing now?" River nearly whispered into the phone, so Jett was probably nearby. Her brother disapproved of Desi's cold-shoulder technique, but then her brother was as arrogant as Tahl. At least he hadn't decreed she choose his lieutenant, but then Jett was more sensitive than that.

"Driving. Thinking. I'll check in later, River. Hug the babies for me, okay?" The one thing about being claimed meant having her own pups, and she was more than ready for that. Her niece and nephew were amazing, even if Andrew made everyone nuts with his precociousness, and Desiree wanted one just like him. *With Tahl's eyes.* Goddamn it. Another country heard from—via the projected thought of her wolf. It paced and whined whenever Tahl was nearby, and the failed to understand that forgiveness—and taking sloppy seconds—wasn't their thing. The silly bitch would take Tahl under any circumstances, but then wolves had no pride and certainly held no truck with possible paranormal influence they couldn't even see.

Tears stung her eyes as River wished her luck and disconnected the call.

The miles melted under the determined press of the accelerator as she ran away. So much for maturing. Thanks to her sister-in-law, she had learned the smart way to manage her financials, and her website business, including the oversight of *Simply Dressed,* meant she was an independent businesswoman. Moderately successful. *And it could all come tumbling down in a few short months when your first heat strikes.*

"And it wouldn't have worried me, not one bit if he hadn't waltzed off after her!" It was okay to say it out loud, here. In the privacy of her car. Because she'd stupidly assumed he would want her too, back then.

She blinked against burning tears. "And I *am* a grown up. Even if I'm running like a child."

Of course, no one commented, not even her wolf.

Desiree couldn't get past the devastating emotions of that day. They simmered just below the surface and short-circuited any meaningful connection with males. It was like she couldn't trust any of them, which was crazy. She knew that, but her psyche, or whatever it was called, didn't. The vignette flashed before her eyes.

"I've come to say goodbye," Tahl announced.

She tensed, foreboding stirring in her belly. But she pretended there was nothing to worry about. "Goodbye? Are you going on vacation? In the middle of this rogue issue? Or are you convinced the situation is stable?"

Tahl glanced at Jett, who lifted a shoulder. "We routed them, and the leader is on the run. But it's not a vacation. Jett's given me permission to leave the pack and head over to Ashton Leaf's territory. I expect to stay."

Her brother had known, and somehow that made everything worse. And River had been there to bear witness after she'd told her sister-in-law about her aspirations where Tahl was concerned. Her starry-eyed, lofty, ludicrous hopes. She felt sick to remember, and hoped she'd schooled her features back then. And she'd asked the question she'd known the answer to, preferring to rip the bandage straight off the wound.

"Who is she?"

Tahl didn't prevaricate. "Peyton. Peyton Leaf."

"The Alpha's granddaughter. Right. She… I remember her."

She'd smiled widely, like she was giving her blessing, for heaven's sake, and could remember her response as if it was yesterday, the only thing she could take pride in. Hiding her devastation with an aloof, "Then I suppose there's nothing to say but congratulations!"

And he'd protested, saying it wasn't a done deal, and she'd somehow been gracious…

"I hope you get what you need, regardless."

Had that been a curse? Had she ruined Tahl's hopes and dreams the way he'd ruined hers, like jinxing him or something? Once the hurt and humiliation had eased a trifle, and it had been after he'd returned to Blue Star—sans mate—that she'd been haunted by the absurd thought.

Except it wasn't so ridiculous when one

considered who her mother was and Desiree's apparent ability to influence the outcome of certain things. She didn't talk about it, though Marlene had noticed. Oh, nothing nefarious. Little things, like telling the obnoxious and handsy supplier of one of their garment lines that he wouldn't keep customers if he continued to renege on production schedules. He'd lost his business license shortly thereafter and fell afoul of the IRS.

And there was the time that she'd been justifiably upset with a partner site, and suggested—via a personal message—that they honor their side of the agreement or find another partner. That site had crashed, irretrievably.

Coincidence, she told herself, ignoring all the other times, all related to things that impacted her negatively. Bad luck. She hadn't influenced Tahl's pursuit of that Peyton Leaf, despite how wrong the female had been for him. She hadn't wished it. No, her power wasn't in her mind, like that girl in the horror movie who had killed everyone at her prom. Desi had to voice her jinxes.

But she hadn't been so much of a child, bent on revenge, that she'd do that to him. Not even subconsciously. Tasting for the truth in that thought, she debated turning off at the next exit and heading home. She'd done enough soul searching. And would stand by her decision to refuse him, because the woman in her might not be vindictive, but she deserved better than being second choice. Her wolf whined and pressed for escape, clearly at odds with her belief—again.

Automatically checking her mirrors, she started, her foot faltering on the gas. A sleek, black Camaro sat squarely on her tail. Heart pounding, hands trembling, she swallowed against a dry mouth and tried, unsuccessfully, to ignore the burst of butterflies in her belly.

She could continue her aimless drive or return home—except he'd follow. She was out in the middle of nowhere, asphalt flowing ahead and behind with nothing but fields and the occasional groupings of bushes on either side. *Great planning, Desiree. Now you've got to pull up your big girl panties and face the music.* She could do it.

Signaling, she eased onto the verge and parked on a conveniently level patch. She shut off the engine and listen to it tick over as it cooled. A few deep breaths and she felt able to face Tahl. Not. Her wolf pranced excitedly and she sent it a nasty message to calm down.

Throwing the door open, she flinched when Tahl caught it, holding it for her as she clambered out, her short skirt making a mockery of any attempt at modesty. She caught his glance as it swept over her legs, and she hesitated. His eyes were pure amber wolf, his features strained and his sensuous mouth set in a straight line. She quailed and he caught her arm, nearly lifting her out and onto the solid surface.

The occasional car barreled past, leaving a faint scent of consumed carbons in its wake, and a semi lumbered by, a swirl of wind tugging at her hair.

"You never run from a shifter. Desiree. Not so overtly. I'm through with you running. My wolf has long since lost patience, and the man can't do this anymore." Even Tahl's voice was different. Not smooth and deep, but a harsh sound, as though he'd swallowed a mouthful of gravel. Like his fangs were showing.

"I was going to Jett and River's. Eventually." His implacable regard both terrified and aroused her. Was this was the part of Tahl he kept under wraps, the piece he released when he shifted? Her wolf scratched frantically within, whining, welcoming, and not at all afraid.

Those tawny eyes flared and she panicked, sensing what was coming. "No. Don't. I can't."

She'd heard about the males asserting their claim, been taught what she might expect, but nothing prepared her for the wave of heat washing over her or the surge of abject need erupting from her core. Wavering on her feet, she closed her eyes against the overwhelming sensation, and Tahl steadied her, drawing her close.

His elevated heartbeat pounded at her senses as she leaned against his broad chest, taking in his familiar smell. Something uniquely Tahl and undertones of bergamot. How long had it been since she'd been within proximity to thoroughly scent him? A sob clawed its way up her throat and erupted past her lips as his pheromones worked their magic.

"Shh. It's okay." His big hand smoothed over her hair. "It'll be okay."

"It'll never be okay." Somehow, she found the strength to straighten and shove at his chest.

Without totally releasing her, his effortless strength apparent, he gave her a little space, staring into her eyes. His wolf simmered, but the verdant green of his iris was back. "It has to be okay. I've claimed you."

"You've triggered my heat," she replied, bitterness coating her tongue.

His handsome face tightened further. "Semantics. You're mine, Desi. I'd have preferred your surrender, but you are so damn stubborn."

"Stubborn? You mean because I've made it clear I'm not interested, you call me stubborn?" It took considerable effort to form coherent sentences.

Something she'd interpret as pain twisted his mouth if she cared to infer anything, and he shook his head. "I hurt you back then, and for that I'm sorry. Truly sorry. But you've let your pride come between us, and I won't allow it."

Maybe she hadn't grown up because she balled her hand tightly and aimed it at his face. His quick reflexes wrapped up her fist and held it at bay.

"You prick. You autocratic bastard." A wave of need belied her words, and she struggled to push it down, hanging on to her indignation by her fingernails. Tahl's nostrils flared and she felt his wolf through his grasp. Hers responded in kind and she couldn't fight them both. Hot tears escaped and tracked down her cheeks as she moaned in terrible, overwhelming desire, sagging against Tahl once again.

"Ah, baby. I'd have picked a better place—"

The faint squeak of brakes and the rolling crunch of tires cut him off and he whirled, tucking her behind him against her vehicle in almost the same motion. A car door creaked and then slammed and she heard the rustle of fabric and the jingle of metal.

"You and the lady having a disagreement?" An authoritative voice broke the silence.

"No, officer. We were on our way to the same place and stopped to chat."

Desiree peered past Tahl's big form and saw an older patrolman, standing squarely in front of them, one hand resting casually on his leather holster. Opaque shades reflected both their distorted images, but surely it was her imagination that her body shimmered in the dual lenses. Though she figured a splash of water would fizzle and evaporate if thrown her way. She bit back another moan and clenched her thighs together.

"Ma'am?"

Her voice was shaky—nothing she could do about it as she wrestled with the pheromones overtaking her system. "Just chatting."

At least a minute ticked by as the cop studied

them, and she could sense Tahl's wolf coiling aggressively. She eased out from behind him so the officer could see her fully. It was imperative he not be exposed to shifter tradition. The other man relaxed his stance a little when she presented herself and gave her a nod.

"Well, best you get back on the road, then. Ladies first. The gentleman and I will exchange a few words. Give you a little time to cool off, if it was more than a chat."

Tahl reached into his pocket and the patrolman stiffened. "I'm going to give her the keys to the cabin, officer." He extricated a set on a chain and passed them over, the jingling sound dragging over her senses with excruciating shrillness.

Cabin? She took the keys with trembling fingers, doing her best not to let their flesh touch. With a nod to the policeman, she slipped into the driver's seat, turning over the engine. Her vision felt off and her head was wooly, stuffed with cotton as she struggled with her seatbelt.

Carefully checking her mirrors, she cautiously pulled onto the highway and accelerated away, Tahl, the cop, and their vehicles, fading into tiny figures set in a frozen tableau.

Her first instinct was to head back to River and Jett's—she couldn't go home. Her mother was unpredictable when it came to shifter tradition, probably because she wasn't one. And yet she'd suggested that her daughter could do far worse than Tahl. What to do?

Light perspiration broke out over her entire body. Her hands slid on the steering wheel and she dried first one, then the other on her skirt. She *needed*, a belly clenching, breast aching, screaming in sexual desperation, and the focus of her need was standing by the road miles back, hopefully not squaring off with a cop. This was so not the way it was supposed to go.

But was it supposed to progress so quickly? She flicked the air conditioning higher and tried to think. She could keep driving, but would eventually have to seek refuge someplace and try to ride out the waves of arousal storming her system. They'd only get worse. And worse. Females coming of age and going into heat on their own could do it, had done it, but she had no idea about those triggered. Her fingers clenched white and she barely stopped herself from wishing bad things on a certain arrogant male shifter. Her wolf whimpered a warning, more than aware that their fates were now tied together.

"Shut up!" She nearly screamed it at her animal and tried harder to focus.

A picture of *the* cabin floated into her head as she sought a turn off to head back toward Blue Star. If Tahl had the keys to the family retreat, then her brother had given them to him. Probably given *her*, with his blessing. She ground her teeth and focused on the betrayal before accepting she'd be meeting her freaking mate at the cabin of her childhood. A nice, isolated place where this insane need could be assuaged and then she'd have a clear brain to think things through. Not to mention bestow that additional talk on Tahl that he'd been craving.

She held it together for the next half hour, taking deep breaths and exerting her considerable will. She was crawling out of her skin by the time she arrived, bumping along the rutted trail that left the rarely used narrow pavement off-shooting the highway.

The keys ground in the lock and the door resisted her initial push. The interior was a little musty, suiting her frame of mind, and she tugged a dust sheet off the couch. Sinking down, she tucked her feet up beneath her and wrapped her arms around herself.

UNDONE BY DESTINY

Her body was nearly too hot to bear her touch,
but she held on tight and waited—thinking.

Chapter Three

After the cop offered some sage advice about the dangers of parking off a busy thoroughfare to "chat", and then graciously waved him on his way, Tahl drove as fast as he dared to the cabin. Desiree wasn't picking up her phone, and there was no guarantee she'd head to the woods, but other than her brother's or her mom's, where else would she go? Unless she ran…

He dismissed that thought outright. No matter how furious she'd be with him, Desiree knew the score and she wasn't masochistic, he didn't think. Her body would be on fire and every minute that passed, she'd be suffering. He cursed his impulsiveness and lack of control, but in truth he'd reacted instinctively to the chase.

Containing his chaotic emotions was difficult, and he focused hard on the blacktop scrolling out ahead of him. His future mate was struggling, and easing her immediate need was his primary goal. She might kill him afterward, and if she didn't, then Jett would. Or River, or Marlene … he didn't doubt there would be a lineup of shifters to contend with, once they heard the story. Losing control on the side of the freaking road!

Her sports car was parked, nose in, to the cabin, and he paused to lean his weight against the driver's door, closing it tightly. Spying her purse on the passenger seat, he cursed, pulling on the handle. Locked. With the keys in the ignition. Could this day get any worse? His wolf pawed aggressively, no doubt pleased that its mate had been so aroused that she forgot the mundane.

Now that he was here, he was stalling, and he grimaced. Nothing much scared him, but the female presumably inside the cabin… He forced his feet to carry up the short set of stairs and opened the front door with a confidence he didn't feel. Until he saw her.

Huddled on the couch, facing him, was his future mate, the most beautiful thing he'd ever seen—or scented. Cheeks flushed, hair now streaming in wild abandon and clothing awry, she glared at him, her rage muted by the trembling need radiating from her tense body.

"Baby. I got here as soon as I could. I—" His attempt at an apology was overridden as Desi lurched to her feet.

"It's not fucking fair that I have no recourse in this. It's a done deal because *you* decided. You. And now I'm stuck with you. I have to submit to your … physical attentions so I can function." She laughed, a harsh mimicry of her usual, musical burst of sound. The one he hadn't heard in his vicinity for a very long time but had never forgotten. The dichotomy scalded his senses.

She stood, her body shaking, the hormonal flux pouring off of her, and he balled his fists to keep his hands to himself. A vastly angry Desiree was an incredibly beautiful and appealing female and his wolf seethed with impatience against her siren call. Tahl shoved his animal back and cudgeled his brain for something that would soothe her. Some sense of self-preservation kept him from offering his heart. It was quite likely she'd carve it out of his chest and eat it with a spoon.

His breath stuttered as with awkward, jerky movements, she yanked at the front of her silky shirt, the fine fabric rending beneath her impatient hands. She threw the remnants in the general direction of the couch before working at the zipper on her little skirt. The garment slid over her thighs to pool around her ankles, his avid stare tracking it as the black lace of her matching panties was revealed as well as the long length of her legs. She stepped out, nearly losing her balance, and kicked the material away.

This was so not how he imagined it. Throat dry, he closed the distance. "Desiree. Easy, baby. Let me—"

"You've done enough, Tahl," she coughed out between shuddering breaths. "Now do what nature intended." Her pretty bra popped open and her breasts were displayed. Sitting high on her narrow torso, they were in perfect proportion to the rest of her, though visibly swollen with need, the dark nipples beaded tightly.

Everything in him screamed to take her right fucking now, his cock so hard it hurt, his wolf groveling. *Groveling.* With inner strength he somehow drew from somewhere, perhaps his conscience, maybe his aching heart, he wrestled his libido into submission and hugged her instead. Trying to offer her comfort. His eyes closed against the intense draw of her soft, silky skin, the heat of her radiating intensely to the very marrow of his bones.

Desiree wrestled free, wild-eyed and flushed. Surely no other male would have been so fucking stupid as to trigger his future mate's heat on the side of a goddamn highway and then leave her unfulfilled? He cursed himself again.

She scrabbled at the fine stuff of her underwear and it met the same fate as her shirt. Tahl drank in his first sight of the female who was his, all creamy skin and smooth curves, the soft dark hair at her apex neatly trimmed. But she was shaking harder, out of control, the scent of her arousal overwhelming him, and instinct took over.

With economic movements, he stripped off his own clothing. Desiree swayed, her eyes tightly shut as she panted through the tiny whimpers falling from her lips. He spoke her name even as he gathered her up and bore her down on the wide, soft couch, but she wouldn't—or couldn't—open her eyes.

There was no time, or need, or foreplay. He'd left her too long. Testing her preparedness with one finger, he grunted his satisfaction. Soaked. Her thighs opened wide for him as he maneuvered between them, her arms splayed and her head thrown back. She writhed, her wolf clearly right at the surface, and her whimpers escalated both in volume and quantity.

Recognizing the time for fucking couldn't be put off by conversation, however necessary, he fit the weeping crown of his cock against her opening. Wet, sultry heat engulfed him as he surged inside on a desperate thrust. And froze at her muffled yelp.

"Fuck me, baby. Fuck. Me." He wrapped her up, working his arms beneath her shoulders to tuck her as tightly against him as he could manage while holding his cock steady, giving her time to adjust. It was his turn to screw his own eyes shut in order to concentrate on not moving one fucking iota. He'd just taken her *virginity*, and even his wolf paused in its desperation to claim her.

Slowly, her tense body began to relax and her breathing regulated, as much as the breathing of a frantic female in heat could calm. In contrast, her sweet pussy clenched around his anxious cock and he ground his teeth not to disgrace himself before he made it good for her.

Cautiously, he withdrew a little then eased back in. Her heat had prepared her body, even if he hadn't, and his movements strengthened into a measured rhythm within the silky wet walls of her sheath. He murmured to her, filthy, sweet snippets he wouldn't have believed himself capable of.

"My darling Desi. Your pussy is so fucking tight, baby. You're squeezing me, stroking me. Hot as the sun.

It's like coming home."

When her hips synchronized with his, rocking in an instinctive rhythm, he breathed easier. He'd hurt her, but she was experiencing pleasure now, and he redoubled his efforts to please her. Grinding against the apex of her pussy, he was rewarded with quiet moans and increasing efforts to take him deeper. He nuzzled her throat but warned his wolf away—he wasn't going to compound his impatience with a bite. He owed her that, to wait until she was in a better space to accept his claim.

With her movements becoming choppy and her cries intensifying, he worked harder to increase pressure on her engorged clit. Deftly circling his hips, he coaxed an orgasm from her. Her response milked his straining cock mid thrust and his drawn-out groan drowned her gasping shriek as she went over. Her pussy clamped around him, repeatedly, as his seed spewed forth. He settled his weight on her, wishing he had claimed her so that their first pup might even now be forming in the depths of her womb.

Withdrawing from her limp body, he got his breathing under control before hustling to the bathroom. He cleaned up quickly before finding a couple of the softest towels. One he soaked in warm water, squeezing it out, carrying it and the other back to her. Gently cleansing between her thighs, he marked the bloody show, and despite his regret for his impulsive actions, couldn't tamp down the bone-deep satisfaction that he would be the only male to ever have carnal knowledge of his mate's beautiful body. He didn't care to consider the implications behind Desiree's purity, the reason why she'd saved herself.

Drying her swollen folds, and then passing the towel over the rest of her to mop up the dew of perspiration coating her skin, he watched her sleep for a moment, keeping his gaze trained on her face. He was ready to take her again, as was the practice with shifters when they claimed their mate, but he was going to deviate from that tradition. He might end up with blue balls, but before he indulged either of them, they were going to have a conversation. Unless Desiree's need circumvented it.

He made his way to the larger of the three bedrooms and quickly made up the bed, taking enough time to ensure the linens were tightly tucked in—he might be trying to do the honorable thing, but he was fully aware the mattress would be seeing some action. He then returned to scoop up his slumbering mate. She'd been released from the initial onslaught of her heat, but it was only a matter of time before she craved satisfaction again. *And would have to accept it from a male she detests—at the moment.*

The enormity of what he'd set in motion made his arms weak as he set her down in a boneless sprawl on the ivory sheets. Had Jett questioned himself when he'd claimed River without so much as a by your leave? That kind of thing had been common in the past when there wasn't time for ceremony or no one paid it any mind. Or at least the males paid it no mind. Tahl drew up the comforter and lowered it over Desiree, fighting with his more evolved self while hearing his wolf growl with contentment. At least one of them was totally pleased, though he supposed Desi's animal was as well. It was far simpler for their wolf counterparts.

He'd had a taste of being powerless, without choices, and he dreaded the morning after when Desiree would likely vent. But what was done was done. He smoothed the long, black hair spilling over the pillow, straightening out the tangles as best he could with his fingers. Tendrils ran through his fingers like silk and soothed his jagged worry.

With a sigh and one last lingering glance at his female, he went to locate his clothing and pulled it back on. The larder was empty so he'd head to the nearest town for supplies. Pick up something for Desiree to wear, as well, seeing as the remains of her clothes wouldn't cut it.

Pausing, he gathered up the fabric remnants to dispose of them—no point in reminding her of how powerless she'd actually been against her need, and would be again. And again. His wolf reminded him that they'd take care of that need as was their duty—and their pleasure—and he slapped the animal down. He could do without simplistic.

He scribbled her a note, though doubted she'd wake for some time. Physically exhausted, for certain, and emotionally drained, Desi would need to recharge.

****

The town was one he wasn't familiar with, the main street relatively free of traffic as he cruised along, looked for somewhere that sold what he needed.

He loaded up his vehicle with all the necessary supplies, shopping mechanically at the small store that was stocked with a surprising array of groceries and dry goods, before asking for directions to a woman's boutique. He always carried a go-bag in the trunk, because as the Alpha's lieutenant he never knew when he'd be required, but he doubted Desi had anything other than the clothes she'd torn off her back. His wolf, acquiescent after the last set down, flexed at the memory, wishing it had had the privilege to disrobe her.

The lady behind the counter gave him a pitying look. "Boutique? You might try the Consignment Trends on the corner."

Blue Star wasn't a big place by any stretch of the

imagination, but this small country town was minuscule in comparison and he supposed people shopped in the larger centers if they wanted a boutique. Thanking her, he found the place almost immediately.

Surreptitiously consulting the tags in Desi's shredded clothing, he managed to find a few things in her size—the important items brand new, heaped in a straw basket on top of a circular rack. He dropped the ruined clothes into a convenient trash can, before worrying that the inquisitive teenager running the consignment store might fish them out. He could envision the interested girl speculating that he'd stolen a woman and torn her clothes off. And done Lord knew what else to her. His actions were was as close to kidnapping in the modern shifter world as anything else, so he supposed it wasn't farfetched thinking.

"Twenty-seven ninety-five." The girl studied the clothing and then him. "You got any shoes to go with this stuff?"

Desi's shoes probably weren't going to match the *stuff*, and he gloomily shook his head.

"What size she wear?"

"No clue." That pretty much summed him up.

"There's some new flip flops in a bin over there. Small, medium and large. Extra-large."

He poked through the contents of the container and conjured up another vision of his mate's feet. Long and slender. He picked out a size large in a shocking shade of pink with little stars dotted over the straps and chose an extra-large pair in yellow with a butterfly embellishment.

"Best take a medium in the green, so as you don't offend her," Miss Practical Upsell said, and he snatched them too. Frogs? "Only two-ninety-five."

They smelled strongly of rubber and plastic as

she tucked them into a separate bag, and he passed over his credit card.

"Cash only, mister."

He offered fifty bucks and while she was making change, plucked a wire hanger from the rack closest to him. "How much for this?"

"What you gonna do with it?"

"I locked keys in a car."

Her cute features scrunched up in thought. "Jimmy at the garage could help. Where you living?"

Right. Pull up to the cabin with Jimmy from the garage right behind him, and exacerbate the total fuck up that was his current situation. The visual made his eye twitch. He stuck the hanger back. "I'm good."

"Nah. It's on the house." She gestured at the rack and he snagged the makeshift jimmy back with a nod of appreciation.

Tossing the sack in with the groceries, he drove back to the cabin, wondering if she was awake. It was getting late and maybe he could put a meal together. The thought of taking care of his mate warmed his belly.

As he was transferring the bags to the porch, his cell buzzed. Jett. Fuck, he should have called. "Sorry, Alpha. We're at the cabin."

A chuckle filled his ear. "My mother couldn't reach Desi. But I figured she was with you and you were making progress."

Good thing someone had faith in him. "It's done. Almost."

"You've claimed her." Was that hostility in his Alpha's voice?

"She's mine," he said, careful to keep any note of defensiveness from his voice.

Jett sighed gustily. "My little sister. I'm fucking ambivalent, Tahl, I don't mind saying, despite giving you my blessing. But hey, man. Welcome to the family, officially."

"Thanks. I think."

His Alpha laughed again. "I mean it, Tahl. I'll pass the word. Take your time coming home."

No way was he sharing his predicament. He'd make this right. "I'll let Desi know her—our—family was asking."

She was still sleeping, in much the same position as he'd left her in. Setting the sack filled with her new clothes on the dresser, he perched beside her for a few minutes, breathing in her scent, listening to her steady, long breaths. Her classic features were beautiful in repose, and so relaxed. He doubted that he would see that particular visage for some time. Regretfully, he shoved to his feet and went to the kitchen.

He'd cobbled together a fairly impressive meal, comprised of a loaded salad, potatoes au gratin—albeit out of a box—and had marinated two fine steaks when he heard her stirring. The "homemade" cherry crumble had been a last minute addition from the grocer's shelf to go with the gourmet vanilla ice cream. He knew Desi's favorite foods, and a full belly wouldn't be amiss.

As badly as he wanted to go to her, he throttled back and waited for her to come to him. Water ran in the back of the cabin while he set the table, and a few minutes later, she hesitantly stepped through the doorway. His gut suddenly roiling, Tahl drank in the view. A threadbare robe swathed her slenderness and trailed to her ankles, probably something Jett had left behind.

She avoided his gaze, staring around the living area. Speaking in a near whisper, she said, "I was looking for my clothes."

"I ... uh, tossed them. They weren't wearable."

"Right."

"I left you some new things in the bedroom."

"Oh. Thanks."

He'd become used to the aloof Desi over the past while, a studied indifference she affected around him. He remembered flirtatious, fiery Desi, someone he was certain still existed under the cold armor. The one who'd cared about him, and not in a sisterly way. But this was uncertain Desi, and he didn't care for it. He moved around the table and pulled her close, feeling her tremble.

Against her hair, he said, "Are you all right?"

She stiffened and pulled away. *Okay, wrong thing to say.* "I'm fine. As fine as being thrust into a brand new stage of my life without being consulted can be fine."

"*Our* life, baby." He might not always choose the right words, but he recognized the need for clarity. It was probably not the time to remind her he'd tried to convince her earlier.

With a miserable glance, she went to the sink and turned the water on. Filling a glass, she sipped at it, keeping her back to him. He knew she was crying and faltered. Tears unmanned him. He grabbed the steaks and put them on the grill, giving her time to compose herself. He'd gladly soothe her but knew she didn't want him near at the moment.

"A few minutes and the meat will be done."

"Sure." She set the glass down and faced him. Aside from a slight reddening of her lower lids, she appeared remarkably composed.

"Why don't you take a seat?" After what they'd recently shared, he sounded ridiculously formal.

"Thanks." Apparently, her previous, bitter statement had reduced her to singular responses.

"We need to talk."

"About what?"

His temper stirred, warring with his effort to make amends. He forked the meat onto a cutting board to let it rest so it would bleed satisfactorily on their plates instead and set it in the middle of the table. Taking the potatoes from the oven, he carefully lowered them to a space equidistant between them, and then went to get the salad from the fridge. "You want dressing? Ranch or Blue Cheese?"

"Blue Cheese. Thanks." *Progress.*

As he took his place, she shifted uneasily in her chair, and he scented faint arousal. "Eat, Desi. I'll bet you haven't had anything much today." He managed not to say that she'd need the energy, not wanting to be the one to bleed on the table, as she picked up her steak knife.

They ate in silence for a few minutes, wordlessly spooning potatoes onto their plates and sharing out the salad. The meat was properly cooked, and consuming the repast kept their attention before he tried again. "Jett called. Maybe you want to speak to him yourself. Or your mom. Maybe River."

"And tell them what? Jett gave you the keys to this cabin. You think I don't know what that means? And River doesn't need a reminder of how a mating *isn't* supposed to play out."

"I'm sorry." He suspected that would be his go-to expression for the next, say, fifty years or more. "Jett will tell them. And your mom."

"Great." She pushed her plate away, wiping her mouth on a paper towel instead of a napkin. Sue him, he'd done pretty well remembering to buy even them.

"Desiree… It's done. Except for the actual claiming."

Her hand lifted instantly to her neck, her slender fingers searching. "Why didn't you get it over with?"

On a deep breath, he said. "Because I want it to mean something to you, other than another necessary part of our connection."

"Well, good luck with that." She caught her breath and pressed a fist against her belly. She doubled over it and whimpered.

"Desi—"

"Stop it!" She pushed up from the table, her chair toppling over and the china rocking with the vehemence of her actions. "Just make this go away, this insane need I have, that you caused. Fix it."

At a loss, he stood and reached out, but she batted his hand aside, turning on her heel to flee toward the bedroom. He followed, catching up with her as she gained the doorway. Catching her arm, he spun her around and shook her gently. "Look at me."

"I don't want to look at you. I haven't wanted to look at you in years. But you just couldn't give it a rest." She sobbed and collapsed against him and he bore her heated weight into the bedroom and tumbled her onto the mattress.

Her obvious arousal shut down any additional conversation and he strove to ignore her outburst. She was obviously hurting and the fact she'd gutted him didn't dampen his desire for her. Stick prick, no conscience and all that.

Shoving the skirt of her robe up around her waist, he made himself take the time to lavish tender kisses on her smooth belly. It was far from a hardship to taste the faint salt of her skin and follow the enticing aroma of her need to her apex. With Desiree moaning and writhing beneath his ministrations, Tahl explored her swollen folds with his tongue. He slid his hands beneath her full buttocks to lift her higher for his touch, feasting on the tender tissue slick with her cream.

When her hands finally found his head, fingers working through his hair, he gave her the orgasm she'd been begging for, her touch soothing his beleaguered wolf. Tahl the man was gratified to hear her scream his name, and he lunged up and over her, one hand scrabbling with his fly to release his howling cock.

Grasping his shaft, he fit in against her pulsing opening and carefully inched inside, aided by her slippery lubrication. She whimpered, but her thighs fell wider and lifted to close around his hips, drawing him deeper. He set his hands on either side of her shoulders, staring into her beautiful face, but her eyes remained closed against him. He lowered to kiss her, but she rolled her head from side to side, panting frantically.

Probably, it was better that way—that he couldn't see into her soul. At least not until the despair he sensed wouldn't be written for anyone to read. Even someone as dense as him. His wolf drove him onward, though he lagged, and he began to thrust with increasingly vigorous strokes.

As she'd done earlier, Desiree met him, her body moving instinctively to increase the friction and their pleasure. His orgasm warned, gathering at the base of his spine.

"Bite me. Please." Her desperate plea registered through his narrowing senses. "Give me a child."

Burying his face in the crook of her neck, he held his release off. Blind need drove him, like his wolf, and he granted her wish. Her tender flesh scored easily beneath his canines, and the instant connection, fuelled by the tangy taste of her blood, shoved him over the cliff of climax.

Desiree screamed, her throat working against the raw sensations before she came again, squeezing his cock tighter than a vise. With a shudder, he collapsed, using the last of his coherence to ease to the side and spare her his entire weight.

As the room came back into focus, he realized he hadn't taken the time to strip down, his wolf mourning the lack of skin to skin contact.

"Baby?" He raised up on one elbow and studied her face. She was asleep again, drained by the intensity of their sex.

The angry mark on her neck glowed, even in the dim light, and while his wolf reveled at the sight, Tahl uneasily intuited that the evidence of his claim could spell the beginning of the end. He desperately hoped that Desiree wouldn't pervert their connection, but knew he had to be prepared for that possibility.

Leaving her to whatever dreams she was immersed in, he rolled off the bed, tucking his sated cock away. He'd deal with the dishes and put away the food, then fetch his go-bag, see if he could get her purse from her car. Shoulders slumped with exhaustion, he made his way to the kitchen. He'd created this mess—all of it—and it was up to him to clean it up.

Chapter Four

Desiree shoved a tendril of hair from her eyes after she pried them open, and then sorted out where she was. The preceding events from the last twenty-four hours slammed into her with enough force to steal her breath. She couldn't shield against them, her head throbbing before the onslaught. Her body echoed and underscored her new reality, her heat like a residual flame, but without the mindless, driving and desperate need that had stolen her control.

Accepting what was done, was done, she parceled up the more debilitating emotions and focused on the practical. Regardless of what some other people thought, she had an analytical brain and the time spent huddled and waiting on the couch hadn't been wasted, even distracted as she'd been by that insane arousal. Her lips twisted when her fingertips drifted over the healing bite on her neck. At least that was over. Tahl had assuaged her need—thoroughly—and his claim was complete. Conception could occur during first claiming, so if she was lucky...

"You're awake." His quiet observation made her start and automatically yank the sheet up to her chin. Not that he hadn't seen every inch of her. Her face flushed at the recollection of stripping for him, begging...

"I'll get up."

"I'm making coffee. Take your time."

Staring after his tall form, she asked herself how he could look so composed. It wasn't fair, none of it, as she'd told him, and she added another tick against him. She was a simmering, sticky wreck, this time her wolf seeking its mate, and he was fresh from a shower, sauntering around without a care in the world.

At least she hadn't lost her shit when he appeared. Enough of the drama. She knew this aloof side of her was pretty fragile, but it was the one she'd shown Tahl since he'd returned and would continue to show him. The outrage she'd expressed was counterproductive, and a volatile Desiree was a vulnerable Desiree. *Not happening.* She clambered from the bed and headed for the shower, taking advantage of the abatement of her heat to think harder about her future, ignoring the sad whimper from her heart.

The needles of the fine spray from the showerhead prickled against her skin as she cleansed her body, saving her hair until last. The tenderness of the junction between her legs made her hiss with discomfort and worked a sly finger beneath the tight wrap she'd put on her feelings, to tug and unravel the bandage. Losing her virginity hadn't been the most pleasurable experience, despite the numbing of her arousal, but she knew Tahl had done his best to make it good for her once he understood.

Lathering her hair, she wrenched her mind away from considering how skilled he'd been, despite the hasty couplings required to dampen her agonizing need. In truth, all her body required was his seed to calm her, but he'd ensured she got hers—two stupendous orgasms, or was it three? With an exasperated huff, she rinsed and felt for the conditioner. She'd never forgive him. Never. No matter how talented he was, sexually. After all, he'd gained that knowledge by— *Nope. Not going there.*

Toweling off, and then shrugging into the robe Jett had left behind on one of his visits, she approached the sack on the dresser. She plucked the garments out, one by one, and winced. It was no accident her mother owned a boutique, and Desi dressed accordingly. All the women in their family were clothes horses, and Desi, in particular, loved sumptuous fabrics and style. The short-sleeved, white blouse was sewn from some blend of fibers she'd never heard of—at least not in that combination—and the little, flirty, pink skirt was… Well, she didn't have the words.

"Wasn't a lot of choices." Jeez. You'd think he was part cat, although wolves could sneak up on their prey too. Not that she was his prey, no matter what he thought. He closed the distance and said, "I brought you a coffee. White, two sugars. And your purse. It was in your car and I thought you might want your phone … and other stuff."

Sweet coffee was one of the few treats she allowed herself, and the fact he knew how she took it might have softened her—if she was in the mood to let him past her defenses. And at the moment she wasn't in the mood to talk to anyone, phone or no phone. She gestured at the skirt and blouse. "Thanks. And the clothes are fine. It's not like I'll be wearing them for long."

Silence stretched, far too long as she heard the words like a distant echo. Color stained her cheeks. She could *feel* the blood rushing to her face, and Tahl grinned, though his eyes were wary. She stared him down. "I meant I'd be changing soon. Into my own clothes. At home."

"Get dressed. I'll make some eggs." Handing her the mug, he sauntered off, the picture of arrogance.

She took a thoughtful sip of her coffee, pretending she hadn't wanted to jump his bones, a flare of heat in her core making a liar out of her. Though she wasn't as—desperate. Not at all. This felt more like the way she usually felt in his presence, though she took care to hide it from him and everyone else. Even herself. So maybe…

When shifters conceived, their heat cycle eased

almost immediately. The bite on her neck flared as if in sympathy with her hope and she closed her eyes. *Please let it be true.* She couldn't keep her guard up around Tahl forever. And if she was pregnant that meant he alone had assuaged her need and there was no need to call upon any single males to assist. Small mercies, this current misguided connection being enough to bear. It was her pride hurting, nothing else, and she'd hang onto that premise and try to turn the situation to her advantage.

Expecting a sports bra, maybe, and a pair of basic white panties, her breath caught when she shook some scraps of lingerie out of the sack. Pale blue with wisps of lace. After tearing off the tags, she stepped into the underwear, skimming them up her legs. They were as light as cobwebs, as was the matching bra, though it had unobtrusive banding to support breasts heavier than hers. Regardless, they didn't begin to compare to the outfit on the bed.

With a shrug, she consigned the mystery to someplace in the back of her mind where she might think on it later. And she most definitely didn't think about Tahl handling—and buying—her lingerie. She pulled on the skirt, tucking in the blouse. Both items fit well, same as the underwear, and she shivered. She didn't like the fact that he also knew her sizes.

Her shoes were going to look ridiculous, but who would see her? Then she spied the flip flops. Thongs. Ugly, rubbery things that went perfectly with the outfit. She slipped on the pink ones, astonished at the comfort they afforded, and regarded her new look. The mirror reflected a woman appearing far younger than her twenty-five years, all artifice stripped away, and it scared her.

"Ready for a hoedown," she muttered, grabbing her purse and scrabbling in its depths for some lipstick and mascara.

Tahl was scrambling eggs—another of her favorites—and she moved to top up her cup. Hesitating, she decided to revert to using her manners and added coffee to Tahl's mug.

"Thanks."

"Sure." She went to the window and twitched the curtain aside, staring out at the view. Totally bucolic, and it kind of soothed her. Not that she wanted soothing. What she needed was a clear and sharp mind to utilize the next several minutes. She could do this. She had to.

"Want to sit in?" Tahl put plates on the table, and she took her place, flashing back to her outburst the night before. Make that two outbursts, followed by … sex. She shoved the memories away.

"How are you?" He sat across from her.

"I'm fine." She took a piece of toast and broke a piece off, and then dipped her fork into the eggs. "Thanks for breakfast."

"I'm domesticated," he said. "Comes from living alone for so long."

Right. He was an only child and his parents were gone. He'd spent a lot of time at her home. Details she'd tried to scrub from her brain and ones she didn't want to recall. Who and what he was, what he'd done, didn't matter. Well, maybe what he'd done recently, but they'd come to that.

"I'm hungry." She ate quickly and he followed suit.

After his last mouthful, he pushed his plate aside. "We need to talk, baby."

Baby. "Can you not call me that?"

His green eyes narrowed. She'd have given anything to have him look at her before he walked out of her life to pursue that bitch. "All right," he said quietly.

"We may be mated, but that doesn't give you license to saddle me with nicknames." She wished she could call that back. It implied that she cared.

His mouth tightened, but not before she saw the pain on his face. "Best you say it, Desi. I'm sure you have something to put out there. Can't blame you, considering my impulsive behavior."

She decided not to draw things out. Tahl could apologize until he was blue in the face, but it changed nothing. She was stuck with him, at least during some times in her life. She wasn't good at math, so hadn't multiplied twelve by twenty minus, say, three times nine months, to come up with the number of possible heats in relation to the number of years females could safely bear young. "I might be pregnant."

"You think so?" He sounded pleased and those sensuous lips widened into a smile. "Your heat—"

"Is on the wane," she interrupted. "At least I think it is. I'm not jumping out of my skin."

It felt horribly embarrassing to discuss it. Stupid, really, considering what they'd done together. And would again, but not for a long time if her prayers were answered. The way he looked at her…

"I don't regret triggering your heat or claiming you, merely the circumstances," he offered. Taking a deep breath, he obviously chose his next words carefully. "Desi, I spoke for you with Jett. I made my intentions clear to you or tried to, but you avoided me, until our conversation yesterday at the boutique. But I believe we were inevitable."

Anger bubbled in her belly and threatened to boil over. She swallowed and somehow stayed in control. Typical arrogant shifter. He'd wanted her, and when she hadn't cooperated… And her brother, the Alpha, had given his permission… Goddamn shifter tradition.

Goddamn destiny. It was too much, and she fiercely wished that people would leave her the fuck alone.

When she was certain she could speak as dispassionately as possible, Desiree met Tahl's stare with her own. "Aside from the fact I gave you no encouragement whatsoever, if fact the very opposite, you triggered my heat."

"You cared for me. A lot. I'm sorry I didn't take notice back then. I want to believe you still feel something. Because I ... care about you."

The old clock ticked quietly on the wall and the coffee maker hissed as the seconds spun out. Her entire being seized up her thoughts like sludge. "What happened at Dawnfall?"

Tahl's handsome face closed up and he shook his head. "I can't share that, baby. Desiree."

"You left the pack." *You left me.* "You were gone for some time and came back without any explanation. Nobody heard from you while you were gone." *Not even me.*

"I was in touch with our Alpha."

She waited for him to say something about maybe having some kind of loyalty to her, but that was wishful thinking. He'd wanted Peyton Leaf, and when it hadn't happened—for a reason that had nothing to do with Desi!—he settled for her, the Alpha's sister. He'd always been close with Jett, and their family, so it probably seemed a good deal. How nice that he *cared* for her.

"Okay. Fine." It wouldn't change anything, anyhow. She didn't respond to his hope that she still cared for him. This was war, and no one gave away state secrets nor armed the other side. She'd keep that ammunition to herself. So what if he'd broken her heart? So what if it hadn't been a teenage crush everyone thought she'd bounce back from? So what if she hadn't allowed another shifter to so much as hold her hand, despite her studied flirting? She didn't want anyone else but Tahl, and now she had him she hated herself. And him.

"Desi—"

"What's done is done. It's not like I get a do-over. But I have the right to demand certain things. Conditions."

That wary look was back, and he shoved a hand through his thick, blond hair. Would their children have his hair or hers? Would she look into a pair of green eyes and be reminded— She gave herself a mental slap. Any child they created would be welcome and loved, certainly by her. She had so much love to give, all wrapped up and stuffed deep down because he hadn't wanted it before. It would be a relief to lavish it on her offspring.

"What are these demands and conditions?"

"I don't want to live with you. I'll get my own place or stay with my mother, though I hope you'll want to be involved in our kids' lives. We'll act civilized around one another. If I'm pregnant, then you don't touch me again until my next heat." She ticked her points off on her fingers.

Aside from a slight tightening around his mouth, he didn't seem affected. His words belied her impression, because, with hardly a pause, he responded, "You'll move in with me. I'll be totally involved in our kids' lives. Acting civilized might be a stretch considering your attitude, but I'll meet you half way. And you forget that sex is a big part of shifter lives, heat or no heat."

"This isn't a negotiation, Tahl. You're not going to play that shifter male card with me like I'm some weak female willing to do as she's told."

"You're not at all weak. That's part of your appeal," he replied amiably, though his eyes were resolute. "But no mate of mine will live separate from me. It's my job to care for and protect you, something I can't easily do if we don't cohabitate."

"And Jett will back you," she accused him, that awful sense of being powerless overwhelming her.

"He will, not that I require it. I'm your mate, ba—Desiree. Until death do us part. As you said, what's done is done. There's no going back and we need to make the best of it."

"You bastard. Can you hear yourself?" She stood, glaring at him. "You touch me outside of my heats and the *death do us part* might come sooner than you think."

He lifted a shoulder. "I won't force you, Desi. I'll count on the chemistry between us to soften your attitude. Now you've had a taste—"

Without thought, she swept her arm across the table, swiping the dishes and condiments to the floor where they made a great shattering noise. His arrogant assumption threatened her fragile determination to forget the sex they'd shared.

Tahl didn't flinch. Instead, he leisurely got to his feet. "I'll allow you that, Desiree. Your life has changed and you feel you have no control. You need some time to adjust. But, not again. Civilized, remember? We'll work our problems out without violence or outbursts."

Through gritted teeth, she said, "I have no control. You plan to rule my life. What? Are you going to beat me into submission?"

"I won't need to beat you, ba—Desiree. Besides, our Alpha has banned corporal punishment. I was thinking more along the lines of domestic discipline. Because, this"—he threw his hand toward the mess on the floor—"isn't you."

It wasn't her. But she couldn't think past his promise to *discipline* her. "Then you fucking well better sleep with one eye open, because if you raise a hand to me…" A light flickered behind her eyes, and she expended enormous energy to rein herself in. For an instant she'd seen herself standing over him, blood staining her hands.

"Desiree?" His face clouded with concern and he stepped around the table to take her arm.

Dismissing the disconcerting image, she shook him off, and said, "I mean it, Tahl. If we have to be roommates you don't want to push me."

He stepped back. "Go get ready, get your purse. I'll pick this mess up. We're going to town to see if they sell home pregnancy tests."

Right. Find out if she was expecting. Shifters threw the pregnancy hormone from day one and human tests worked well for them. And if she wasn't… She shivered. Then he'd fuck her again until this heat cycle ended. And during the next. Not finding the idea abhorrent made no sense, but then she had no choice when in heat. That's all it was. And her *plan* had been knocked aside without even a vague consideration. Well, too bad if shifters were all about the sex in between times. She hadn't died, doing without, and having had a *taste* meant nothing. Tahl would just have to learn to deal with it, the jerk.

Moving with as much dignity as she could manage, already regretting outburst number whatever, she used the bathroom and remade the bed. Their combined scents wafted from the sheets and her eyes drifted shut, involuntarily transported on the olfactory memory. Had he slept beside her? Held her? Moisture squeezed from beneath her lids and she blinked rapidly. Crying solved nothing. She'd shed buckets-full over Tahl and there was no point in wasting any more.

He was tying off a garbage bag when she returned

to the kitchen, and she paused to admire the flex in his forearms before chastising herself. She hadn't allowed herself to really look at him since his return. There wasn't any need, considering that his tall, muscular frame with his thick blond hair and discerning green eyes was emblazoned in her head, right down to the tiny dimple in his left cheek. She knew his scent, could recognize him by the way he moved, and despite her efforts to expunge other personal knowledge about him, likely knew him better, or as well, as Jett. That he now had carnal knowledge of her and effectively owned her could have been the happiest time of her life. With a grimace, she composed herself.

"Ready?" He didn't reference the pile of dirty dishes in the sink or anything else related to her acting out, and she again resolved to keep things under wraps unless he pushed her. With an inner snort, she accepted her ability to control herself around him—her mate—would be sorely challenged. But if he touched her... She closed that down. Because if he touched her outside of her heat cycles, when she couldn't pretend her response was purely biological, she'd lose all of herself. So, no unnecessary sex. *Shut up, wolf.*

"Desiree?"

"Huh? Oh, sure. Sorry. Just thinking. I'm ready."

"Okay if we take my car?"

After his oh-so-lordly attitude a few minutes earlier, she recognized a concession when she heard one. He knew she preferred to drive. "That's fine."

He held all the doors for her and ensured she was buckled up before heading toward town. Viscerally aware of his proximity, she leaned away and stared out the window.

"You were a virgin."

Did he think he was safe within the confines of a

vehicle barreling down the narrow road? Was this was a continuation of his assumption that he'd turned her into some addict craving sex like chocolate? She took a deep breath. *No more outbursts.* "Yes."

"I wish I'd known."

Uh huh. That was a conversation they could have had for sure. *Hey, Tahl. Just so you know, when my brother hands me over to you, take it easy. Because I wasn't.* "It doesn't matter."

"It does to me."

"And you're the important one here."

He threw her a glance before turning onto the short road running through the town. "I'm trying, Desiree."

"Then quit. Okay? There's no need to try. I mean, why bother?"

"Because you've made up your mind not to, is that it?" He pulled up in front of what looked to be a grocery store, and turned the car off, returning both hands to the wheel. His knuckles showed white and she understood how hard she was pushing him again, not that she gave a damn.

"Civilized doesn't include discussions about my personal life, and if anyone can talk about making up their mind…"

Eyes blazing emerald fire, he stared at her. "We're mated. Everything about you is of interest to me."

She released her seatbelt and grasped her purse, ignoring his anger and the way it made her belly clench. "I don't see it that way."

Grasping her arm, he said, "I was honored to be your first."

"And my last, unless death does us part." She flung the door open and wrenched free, stepping out. A hoarse curse floated out behind her and she slammed the door on it.

No way was she telling her reasons for being a virgin shifter at nearly twenty-five. He was surprised at that fact and should learn not to judge a book by its cover. And she certainly didn't want to feed his ego. Her cell vibrated and she dragged it out as Tahl levered his tall frame out of the car. She peered at the screen in the bright sunlight. River. She wanted to talk with her friend, but not until she could calm herself, so she ignored the call.

Desiree didn't have any close shifter friends other than her sister-in-law, anymore. Her childhood friend, Josie, had been claimed by Max. He'd been her choice and Desi was really happy for them, when she wasn't being reminded of what she was missing out on, which was constantly. So while she kept in contact and was always made welcome in their home, their interaction had dwindled.

As for the paucity of other female friends, it was partly because of who her brother was. Being the Alpha's sister, it made the females either suck up to her or give her a wide berth. And many of them she avoided because they'd been the recipient of Tahl's attentions. If it hadn't been for her human friends, life would have been pretty darn lonely, and even then a fair number of them had older sisters who "knew" Tahl. Manwhore.

She was furious with herself that she'd allowed him to influence her life to such a degree but hadn't managed to do anything about it. Yet she'd lusted after him, wanted him. What did that infer? She knew it made her *feel* even worse.

He held the door to the store open, and she clomped inside, not sparing him a glance or thanking him. She was tired of everything and wanted to get it over with.

"Hello." A middle-aged woman smiled at her and nodded to Tahl. "Welcome back. Did you forget something?"

He was going to ask this woman if the store carried pregnancy tests. She knew it. Interrupting, she asked, "Do you have painkillers?"

"Yes. Two aisles over."

"Thanks." Desi hurried over and scanned down the products. There was a surprising array of over-the-counter medications and on the opposite side were the hygiene and the feminine products. Beside those were "family planning" choices, along with pregnancy tests. She picked one of each, chose a bottle of ibuprofen and made her way to the till.

With a slightly raised eyebrow, the woman checked her out and tucked her purchases into a sack. Tahl brooded in the doorway and she studiously ignored him.

As she made her way outside, he murmured, "Ever independent, baby. I expect it'll take a little time to accept that you don't have to do everything by yourself."

Without deigning to answer, she went straight to the car. He insisted on opening the door again and nearly handed her inside, but she refused to appreciate his chivalry. Tahl had always been a gentleman, but it was lost on her now. Especially when she knew it hid that caveman persona she'd recently witnessed. A few years ago it would have made her hot, but at her age now, not so much.

Clutching the bag, she maintained her silence while Tahl commented on the passing scenery. She could almost pretend they were an old married couple, together for eons. She nearly ground her teeth into dust.

Without giving him a chance to come around and

help her out, she clambered from the vehicle and nearly ran into the house in her desperation. Locking herself in the bathroom, she read through the instructions and used both of the tests. A knock startled her as she set the strips on the edge of the sink to dry.

"Desiree?"

"I'm waiting."

"Open the door."

She didn't want to. She didn't want to share the moment with him and wondered how long she could stall. But being a total bitch really wasn't her, so she grudgingly opened up. He stepped inside, crowding her, and she felt as though all the air had been sucked out of the space.

They both stared at the innocuous strips of paper until first one, then the other developed the sign that confirmed he was as virile as he looked. She was torn between feeling resentful and being ecstatic about having a child. With him. Her happiness wavered, and she struggled to get a grip. This baby didn't deserve to experience even a hint of its parents' angst.

His arm slipped around her shoulders and he dropped a kiss on the crown of her head. "I'm thrilled, baby. I'll confess I might have wished for more time with just the two of us, but having a pup—"

"Please save that endearment for the pup," she said sweetly, gathering up the strips and dropping them into the garbage where they fluttered to land on top of the boxes.

She thought he sighed. "No endearments, Desiree."

It was a victory, but a hollow one, and she well knew it. However, she pasted on a smile and stepped away to head into the bedroom. Finding a laundry bag, she stripped the bed, wondering why she'd wasted her time making it that morning. Had she hoped to christen it again? With a snort directed at her wolf, she rammed the linens into the sack.

"I take it you want to head back to Blue Star."

Without looking at him, she nodded. "No reason to stay here."

A chilly silence unfurled, but she kept her attention on tying off the laundry. Finally, he answered, "The kitchen needs cleaning and then we can go."

"I'll do it. You head back. With two cars—"

"I'm not returning without my mate, Desiree. We're going to stop in to see our Alpha and the family to share the news in person. And then I'll help you pack. The sooner you get settled in my home, the better."

"Well, then. You've got it all figured out." Pushing past him, she stalked into the kitchen.

"Desiree."

Pretending she hadn't heard, ridiculous, considering her shifter hearing, she ran water in the sink and began to scrub the dishes she hadn't broken. She could barely see what she was doing for the impotent tears clouding her vision.

A hard body trespassed into her space, and she caught her breath when he leaned into her. Warm breath washed over her temple. "I'm doing what's best for us. Can you give me your trust in this if you can't find it in your heart to forgive me yet?"

Scrubbing furiously, she chose her words carefully. "I'm not going to pack up all of my former life, and don't ask me to trust my heart to you, Tahl. Ever. As for living with you, I'll be a good roommate."

A heavier gust stirred her hair, and then he stepped back. "I'll put the laundry and the garbage in the trunk."

Chapter Five

That had actually gone better than expected, even if her last comments had punched him in the sternum. Desiree had been independent far too long, and not in a good way, at least not for a possessive shifter male. He had no intention of interfering in her business or asking her to give up her friends, but he'd help her whenever he could. He frowned. The only females she hung around with were humans. And River. Funny he hadn't noticed that before. But then she'd always had lots of males dancing attendance on her, despite the fact she'd obviously never taken any of them up on it. And that interest was past tense. Not that he worried about fidelity. No shifter had cause to worry about that, once mated.

Despite the reassurance, he felt the pinch of jealousy. Centuries back, according to the tomes, male shifters—and a few females—acted on that vile emotion to free up a mate. Maybe it was a blessing in disguise that Desi didn't seem to care about his earlier conquests beyond her interest in Peyton.

With a grimace, he heaved the bags into the trunk. Nope, shifters didn't cheat, but that didn't mean they always lived together happily. Not always. But a high percentage were good together and many were love matches over and above the lust that drove them. Too bad he and Desiree seemed to fit in the first category. But, he wanted her, and no one else, and he'd live with the choice. Surely time would soften her and she'd come to accept him as her mate past the biological imperative.

The front door slammed and she stepped down the stairs in those silly pink flip flops, her own high heels dangling from her fingers. She made the cheap, casual clothes look spectacular, wearing them with a flair he knew the other females envied. Perhaps that was why she didn't have friends.

She strode to her car, digging in her purse for her keys. He wished he'd kept them, made her come to him and pay for them with a kiss. They hadn't even exchanged that form of intimacy, and his gut churned when he remembered how she'd turned her face away despite the overriding heat. *Fuck.*

"I'll follow you," he called.

Desiree slanted him a look he couldn't read, but nodded and lowered herself into the driver's seat. The engine turned over with a powerful rumble and he hustled to start his own vehicle when she backed out with a flourish and was on her way.

Cursing, he followed and caught a glimpse of her bumper glinting in the sun as she hurtled along. Another disagreement was in the offing. His mate had to be more careful. He caught up to her on the highway and was heartened when she drove only slightly above the speed limit.

Had she really thought they would live separately, with him "dropping by" to assuage her heats? She sought to wrest back the control and that wasn't an option, not for him or for most males. He knew she planned to avoid him physically, so he'd have to rely on good, old-fashioned seduction. Tahl's biggest contribution to the pack, to his Alpha, was his stubborn determination to complete any task assigned to him. Desiree might think she was equally determined, but he was going to win this war. There was simply no other option.

When he pulled up beside her at Jett and River's, he was forced to wait while she busied herself with her purse. He suspected she was composing herself and gave her a minute.

Emerging, he marked her pallor as well as her resolution. "C'mon, Desiree. They're family."

"Readymade," she muttered and moved past him to mount the stairs. He winced. She likely knew how much he craved belonging, and the comment, whether it was a deliberate jab or not, found its target.

Jett welcomed them, saying River wasn't feeling well and would join them shortly.

"Is it the baby?" Desiree's voice was full of concern and she peered past her brother. Shifter females weren't immune to morning sickness, though tended to have easier pregnancies than humans.

"I suspect so." Jett shrugged, but he looked worried despite the casual gesture. He grasped Tahl's hand. "Congratulations."

"Thanks." He couldn't hide his ebullience, despite the circumstances.

"Tahl got himself a wonderful mate, Desi."

She sidestepped her brother as he moved to hug her. "As you say, Alpha. I'm going to check on River."

They both stared after her. Jett said, "I take it things didn't go well."

"No. But I claimed her and … she's pregnant."

"Holy shit! You trying to show me up?" Jett clapped him on the back. "That doesn't happen often."

"She wanted a baby. Badly." He needed to share the circumstances of the claiming, and did so, outlining it as briefly as possible.

To his surprise, Jett gave a pained chuckle. "A royal fuck up, Tahl. I can only imagine it. I was nearly as out of control with River." He sobered. "Was she okay? River had to wait for consummation and it was hard on her."

Maybe his Alpha wasn't going to punch him in the face, after all. "She was … anxious. But that's not why she's so angry. With the both of us."

"I can guess. She thinks I gave her to you."

"You did, in granting me permission, and because I triggered her heat without telling her…"

Shaking his head, Jett replied, "She'll come around. Better you, who cares about her and never gave up on her, than one of those single males who've been sniffing around."

"Like Kris," Tahl growled.

"Kris? Not my favorite guy, but he's got his sights on Moira. One of the females we rescued from the rogues."

"I hadn't noticed."

"It's a fairly recent development. But there are others interested in Desi. A couple have indicated their intentions and asked my permission, but you've always been my first choice."

"I'm not hers, Jett," he said ruefully, though intensely grateful he'd pressed his claim when he had. "At least not anymore."

"You've always been her first choice, so get over it. Desi needs a firm hand. Even as Alpha I haven't been able to curb her need for speed and she tends to flout tradition that I can't see changing, no matter how modern the pack is getting. Like her preference for humans. I can leave that up to her mate to help temper her."

"Probably a good thing neither of our mates are around to hear this conversation."

"River wouldn't like it," Jett agreed cheerfully. "Particularly the claiming aspect. But she's accepted that until we can come up with another form of … courtship, for lack of a better word, it's what we have. Destiny."

Tahl was feeling undone by destiny and he was sure Desi felt the same way. He manned up and decided to quit whining, now he'd come clean with his Alpha.

Next, he'd take his mate to see her mother and then head home. Give her time to catch her breath before the Council and the rest of the shifter community was advised. The idea of living with her, waking up to her every morning and seeing her when he came home after work made his heart swell.

"Hello, Tahl." River looked a bit wan, but she was dressed and moving well, so he counted that as a good thing.

"Are you okay?" Jett asked the question before he could, wrapping an arm around his mate's shoulders.

"I'm okay. I didn't sleep well last night and this baby is giving me a bit of grief. That's all it is. I'm grateful the kids are having a rare nap." She smiled at her Alpha before turning her attention to him. The happy look on her face faded a little. "Congratulations."

"Thanks." He dared a glance at Desiree, but she gave him nothing, her expression composed and aloof.

"Jett told me yesterday you were mated and Desi shared the other news. I can't wait for a niece or nephew."

The cool customer who was his mate stepped closer to squeeze River's hand. "Me neither. I always wanted children."

He stood there, feeling like a means to an end, which was, no doubt, precisely what she intended. Biting back a groan he said, "Happy to be of *service*."

Twin, pink lines painted her cheekbones. "We have to see my mom, River, and then I'm moving into Tahl's house."

"Marlene's on a buying trip, Desi. She left early this morning."

His mate paled, and his gut twisted. This was Marlene's comment on their union, and he hated that it hurt Desi, though he knew it was because his mother-in-law had intuited he'd flouted her advice. He could live with her disappointment, but it didn't need to include Desiree.

Without a knife to cut the tension, he moved to lightly grasp her arm. "Let's get going. Give River some time to rest up. We can invite everyone over for dinner in the near future."

With a sickly sweet smile, she said, "Tahl's a great cook."

River came over to hug her. "I'd like that. But don't be a stranger."

"I won't."

He felt the fine tremor beneath his hand as he guided her out to the car. "You okay to drive?"

"Yes."

"I'll see you at your place. If I can't keep up."

Was that a flicker of amusement he caught? He looked closer, but she was back to aloof Desi.

"Okay."

He saw her into her car and they embarked on yet another drive. Separately. Desi's heat might have waned, but both he and his wolf weren't getting the message. Merely touching her arm had made his cock stir, and he'd detected telltale signs that she wasn't immune. He bent his mind to formulating a plan to get her into his bed willingly tonight.

****

"There." She closed the closet in his spare room and stepped back.

Tahl leaned against the wall, secretly fascinated with all the *stuff* his woman had. She'd filled her car and his to the brim. Even checking out the passenger window had entailed compressing a variety of bags piled nearly to the roof, and her sports car nearly burst at the seams.

At first, she'd dithered, clearly uncomfortable

with leaving her home. He'd pulled out a few cases from her room to encourage her, and found himself sent out for boxes shortly thereafter. At least while she was packing she didn't treat him to any of her loaded barbs.

"Finished?" She started, as though she'd forgotten he was there, talking to herself.

"That's the last of it."

"Your clothes are here." And in his closet too. "What about your other things?"

"Like?

He shrugged. She was talking to him, at least, and he wanted to prolong the encounter. "Female stuff. Not your perfumes and makeup, or your bath items. Pictures and things like that."

"They're in the boxes."

"I want you to make your mark here, ba—Desi. Make my house ours."

A look of despair flitted over her features. "Can you stop pushing, Tahl? Please?"

Shoving a hand through his hair, he turned on his heel and headed to the living room. He ignored the neat stack of boxes along the way and chastised himself. He *was* pushing. He'd envisioned this moment for months and was only too ready to have her living in his home, with him. She hadn't had the luxury to prepare. He'd only thought having the familiar around her would help.

He heard her in the kitchen, rustling around, and nearly reached for the remote before appreciating the cliché. With a rueful grimace, he joined her. She had a bag of pasta on the counter and was stacking some fresh mushrooms and onions alongside a carton of milk.

"What are you making?"

"Pasta primavera, or my version of it."

It was near torture to stand so close, and he surreptitiously sniffed the bouquet that encompassed his mate. Pure female with overtones of nature—grassy notes and citrus. An ever-so-faint hint of arousal…

"Are you sniffing me?" She edged away and regarded him with exasperation.

"Maybe." He poked at the mushrooms, noting their slightly wrinkled appearance. "We should probably get in some fresh produce."

"I'll do that tomorrow."

"Uh, thanks. I appreciate it."

She didn't respond, chopping vegetables with considerable skill. He watched the knife flash and of course couldn't help himself. Couldn't leave well enough alone. "You're pretty calm, considering."

Her long lashes flickered as she focused on him. "What did you expect? That I'd sulk in my room? Hide away?"

"Maybe."

"I might be a captive, Tahl, but I promised I'd be a good roommate."

"You're more than that."

"I'm not going to argue." She commenced to whisking butter and flour in a pan.

He'd be frustrated if he hadn't scented her sexual interest. His Desi couldn't blame her heat for that tempting fragrance and he celebrated the awareness. Deciding to bide his time while taking every opportunity to invade her space and capitalize on the attraction, he merely nodded.

"Jett and I have business tomorrow, so I'll be gone all day."

"Sure." She was obviously determined not to take any interest in his life, likely because he'd shut her down on the one question she'd asked. The one he couldn't answer.

"What are your plans?"

"I'll open the shop and help out Michelle if it gets busy. Otherwise, I'll work on my sites from the … from my new home office." His spare room would hopefully serve her well in that endeavor.

"When do you expect your mom back?"

She faltered in pouring milk into the pan. "Whenever she feels like it, I expect."

He slipped his arm around her narrow waist, ignoring how she stiffened. "I'll talk to her. She's pulling away from the family more and more."

Turning, she escaped his hold and went to the counter. "You don't need to do that. My mother has an opinion on everything and I don't let it get to me anymore."

He was still going to have a chat with Marlene. "Anything I can do?"

"Nope. I'll drain the pasta in a few minutes."

"I'll set the table then." He grabbed the appropriate cutlery and plates, handing her a colander while he was at it. They worked in silence and he relaxed a little more. Mealtimes might signify at truce of sorts because Desi was sleeping in his bed tonight, and every night. And he wasn't looking forward to that battle.

****

Under vastly different circumstances, it wouldn't be a hardship sharing a meal with Tahl. She'd found her way around his kitchen fairly easily, likely because she had spent a lot of time in it, growing up. After all, she'd known the man all her life. Until she hadn't.

A curious sense of well-being eased her further, and she wondered if it was because she was pregnant, though barely. She refused to give any credibility to her wolf's purring suggestion that she was contented because she was mated to the male she'd coveted—all her life. Her ire hadn't abated, curled and simmering in the back of her mind, heavily laced with the bitterness of betrayal and insidiousness of guilt.

Thus far Tahl hadn't pushed her, with the exception of following through on his edict that she move in with him. Considering her role as the Alpha's sister, she supposed there would be repercussions if they lived separately, now that she could think coherently. Mustn't let down tradition.

"This is great, Desi." Tahl forked pasta and actually closed his eyes when he chewed.

She wanted to roll her own. Basic sauce, store-bought pasta and some crab she'd discovered in the crisper—hardly a gourmet meal. But she knew he was trying to connect, and despite her ambivalence, breakfast had been a long time ago, and she was hungry again.

Resolving not to give him any reason to invade her space again, considering the way he continued to affect her, heat or no heat, she concentrated on the meal and conversed when necessary. A part of her, the one that had been in lockdown for years, scrabbled at the cage door, encouraged by her wolf. *Let it go, Desi. It may not have gone the way you dreamed, but Tahl is yours… Forever.*

The creamy pasta turned to paste on her tongue. She and Tahl were a mated pair, but at what cost? She'd never be grateful for half a loaf and she couldn't shake the niggling feeling that she'd jinxed the union he'd actually sought with Peyton Leaf. Instead, for some reason, he'd settled for her.

Sure, she was attractive. She wasn't going to retreat behind false modesty—Tahl was interested in her physically, and they'd been friends of a sort growing up. He and Jett had been best friends, and she and Lizbeth had been included by default. Tahl was enamored with her family and now he was truly bound to it. A surge of sadness, mingled with self-pity, overtook her and she pushed her plate aside.

"Not hungry?" He was watching her with those beautiful emerald eyes and for a moment he took her breath away.

"I'm full," she lied and tried to divert him. "I'll clean up and then I have some work to do. A couple of sites I'm managing are due for updates."

"I'll do it. I should have realized you'd get behind. The timing wasn't great."

Anger overtook the sadness and she welcomed it. He just didn't get it. "The timing would never have been great, Tahl. Excuse me."

The palpable weight of his gaze followed her as she left the room to make her way to her makeshift office in his second bedroom. And where she intended to sleep. She cast a glance around. His home was clean and tidy for a male recently single, but screamed "man cave". Her "stuff", still in the boxes, would go a long way to making it her home as well, but she couldn't bring herself to do it.

Immersed in the screen, she started when Tahl's warm hands settled on her shoulders and worked gently at the stiffness there. "It's late."

"I'm nearly finished," she managed to say, past the comforting—and titillating—massage.

He continued to rub and knead despite her efforts to avoid his touch, easily thwarting her movements. "Good thing. Long day."

Reminded of the events of the day, damn him, she clicked through the menu, saving as she went and then powered down. "Satisfied?"

He backed off as she turned to face him, lifting a hand as if to ward her off. "Trying to look out for you, is all."

"You're trying to control me, and every goddamn aspect of my life is what you're trying to do." She choked down the other things she wanted to say. Her wolf was whining, reminding her that no one had tried to take care of her in a long time. *Because you held them at bay, from River to Jett to your mother.*

Sorely conflicted, she resolved to fight this battle when she wasn't so exhausted, and said, "Sorry. I am tired."

"Then come to bed."

"I'm sleeping in here."

"You're in my bed, Desi, whether I have to sleep with one eye open or not."

The implacable Tahl was back. Jett's lieutenant, ruler of his own household, and that included her. She had no doubt he'd put her in his bed, maybe tie her there if she resisted.

"Any other edicts I should know about? Like a curfew? You planning to choose the people I associate with, maybe?"

Regret flashed across his handsome features. "I'll do whatever is right for you. My mate. And the pup you're carrying. I would hope you won't fight me on it." *Because I will win.*

She read the unspoken words in his eyes and heard them in her gut. "Sure. Fine. You keep telling yourself that."

Ignoring the way he stiffened, she lowered the lid of her laptop and levered to her feet. To her chagrin, he didn't concede her any space and she had to deke around him, hustling to the dresser. Keeping her back to him, she rummaged for the flannel pajamas she kept for the rare occasions when she didn't feel well and required the comfort and warmth.

Making her way to the bathroom, she closed and

locked the door. Tahl should consider that stress wasn't good for a pregnant mother and the baby. Her hands trembled as she went through her nightly routine, the familiarity soothing her nerves somewhat. Dawdling as long as she dared, stroking the brush through her hair one last time, she studied herself in the mirror. Her unhappiness was tangible, evident in her eyes and the set of her mouth. With a sigh, her chest again a tight knot of emotion, she went to Tahl's room.

He was already in bed, the linens pooled around his waist, sculpted chest on view. A whorl of scar tissue twisted from the base of his neck and over one broad shoulder, something she hadn't noticed before. And curious, seeing as shifters healed well after injury and rarely scarred, at least not so obviously. But she'd never ask, never do anything to indicate her interest.

Clearly naked under the bedding, the suggestive draping over his hips made her core heat and blanked her mind to anything else. She averted her gaze, but not before noting what a handsome specimen he was—and that he was ensconced on the side of the bed she normally chose. Could she ever catch a break? She willed her inadvertent arousal down.

He set the book he was reading aside and twitched back the covers for her, the gesture more inviting than she cared to accept. She slipped into bed and curled up on her side, facing away from him and drew up the sheet. Already too warm, she resigned herself to an uncomfortable night, with Tahl radiating additional heat clear across the expanse of the king-size bed. It figured he'd have such a huge mattress, the better to practice all the sexual shenanigans she overheard, touted by the females he'd pleasured.

"Sleep well, Desi." The mattress dipped as he leaned over to drop a kiss on her hair.

"Uh huh." It would be so easy to roll over and kiss him for real, actually taste him. But that intimacy was never going to happen. She'd watched *Pretty Woman* often enough as a teenager to know she'd unravel.

Tahl moved away and a click registered before the room plunged into darkness. She hoped he lay awake from unrequited lust and suffer mightily in the throes of it. She stared into the black until her eyes adjusted to the ambient light and she could pick out the various components of the room. It was going to be a very long night.

Her eyes popped open as she registered the solid warmth plastered against her—although, in truth, she'd trespassed well into enemy territory. Tahl's long, muscled body pressed into her softness, and to her embarrassment, she'd slung her leg over his hip. The hard bulge resting on her thigh testified to an enormous erection. Even in his sleep, he was ready to fuck.

Never a sound sleeper, Desiree found it confusing that she'd gotten even a wink of rest, considering the situation, but now was not the time to ponder. Fighting the need to stiffen and perhaps alert him that she'd awakened, she faked a murmur and rolled onto her back. Before she could begin the process of inching away to put more distance between them, he chuckled and hitched onto his side. Propped up on one elbow, he loomed over her and she felt the flurry of his warm breath.

"You talk in your sleep, Desi. And cuddle so sweetly."

She could hardly say she must have been seeking his warmth, dressed as she was in the flannel pajamas. "Sorry. I'm not used to sharing a bed."

"Not complaining." He lowered his head and

sniffed along her temple. "You smell great."

So did he, musky, with that spicy undertone of bergamot. With an effort, she didn't fill her lungs. "I'll let you get back to sleep."

"Desiree." He pressed his lips unerringly in the hollow of her throat, his shifter vision hardly requiring more than ambient light. The touch was gentle, yet possessive and she shivered, her nipples tightening in response and her core heating.

Her wolf begged her to surrender, the animal clearly game for activity outside of the parameters Desiree had set. Beleaguered, she struggled to make her languid limbs move, to say something to make him back off. Except she didn't want to, blaming the residual depths of slumber she'd somehow embraced despite her antipathy for the sleeping arrangements.

"Tahl, I told you…" Her voice held nothing of the firmness she wanted to portray, and she lost it completely when a big, warm hand slid beneath her pajama top to stroke her ribs.

Teasingly close to the underside of her breast, she marked his strong, callused fingers and heated palm. She wanted to squirm, to wiggle herself into a better position where that hand could cup her aching flesh and tease her beaded nipple. Unbidden, her body did just that and he accommodated her, closing around her right breast as a sound of reverence broke from his lips.

"Perfect, baby. I neglected these." He swept his hand over to hold the other mound, fingertips plucking the hardened tip.

The reminder of their hurried coupling tainted his touch, and she stiffened. Tahl's sharp breath told her he'd noticed and even as she parted her lips to protest, he shoved her top up and lowered his head. The hot, wet warmth of his mouth engulfing her breast effectively scattered her thoughts.

Was that her moaning? Making those needy sounds? She writhed, her hands finding his thick hair to work her fingers through the length, as his tongue alternately swirled and lashed a nipple before sucking hard. When he abandoned one breast to administer to the other, she found the will to protest. But not that he stop. She wanted this, wanted to be able to participate in hot, no-holds-barred sex without a biological need driving her. Wanted to have the choice. Feel it.

Her apex was melting with desire, her pussy vibrating with anticipation as she arched against Tahl's mouth, holding him close. He gave a last, lingering lick before trailing his tongue slowly over her quivering belly. A nibble, a tiny kiss … he sensuously tortured her in making a path to her mound, only to be foiled by the waistband of her bottoms.

Tahl knelt. "Lift up, baby."

She hitched her pelvis upward and he efficiently stripped her bare. The sharp, tart scent of her arousal perfumed the air and she heard him growl.

"Fucking amazing."

Her thighs fell wide as he dropped down and laid his head against her. Knowing he was breathing her in, imprinting her need on his senses, unleashed another rush of her cream. He'd slipped past her edict about no sex unless she was in heat, and she was lost in a different form of powerlessness. That of surrender.

She had but a moment to question her sanity before he descended on her swollen folds with the intensity of a starving wolf. His talented tongue explored the sensitive flesh, every nook, and crevice while ignoring the tiny bundle of nerves that required it the most.

"Please, Tahl." Tugging at his hair and then

pulling it had no effect. "I need…"

A wet chuckle resonated before the flat of his tongue swiped a blazing trajectory right *there*. A gentle pinch of her clit pulled her release from the depths of her belly to flood her pelvis and explode over her core. Her toes curled painfully. Tahl suckled, prolonging the sensations and she cried out in overwhelming pleasure.

Instantly, he soothed her with a tender kiss and eased upward to cover her body, grounding her in the moment. "Shh, baby. It's okay. You're okay."

As she came back to herself, she registered his throbbing hardness. He could have pushed his cock inside of her. There was no way she'd have protested, lost in the whiteout of climax. But he waited, wordlessly asking permission.

Her hand crept down to touch her first cock. Damp and hot, silk over steel, it pulsated at her touch. Stroking him gently, she marked the increase in his breathing and the way he pushed into her hand.

"I love your touch, baby," he groaned.

Hesitantly, she tried to position him and he moved to facilitate her effort. The broad crown seemed to find her opening easily and he pressed inside, opening her. The initial resistance her body afforded made her catch her breath and he stilled.

"Okay?"

"Yes." She really had no idea, but it was only fair he receive his own pleasure after bestowing it on her. If she closed her eyes tightly, she could pretend all the ugliness of the past couple of days hadn't taken place, and that she was back in the day when Tahl was all she wanted. All she had eyes—and heart—for.

Inching ahead, she felt him fill her, stretching the walls of her channel until he was fully seated. She let herself simply *feel* as she adjusted, and he began to move, slowly thrusting forward, only to retreat. Her hands rested on his shoulders, tracing their inherent strength.

He worked one arm beneath her back, his other hand cupping the nape of her neck as he lowered to take her lips. The initial brush of his mouth flicked some kind of switch, and she turned her face away. The implied intimacy was like a dash of cold water in reminder, and guilt gnawed insidiously.

Stiffening, he carefully withdrew, recognizing the rebuff, if not the reasoning behind it, and she bit back a protest at the loss. But he effortlessly flipped her and drew her hips upward with a firm grasp. One big hand again covered her neck to press her upper body into the mattress and the heat of him blanketed her.

Open to him, he probed between her folds and with a satisfied grunt pressed home. His girth took her breath and she was helpless to do anything else but take him, her role changed from that of a participant. His cock worked differently deep within her, rubbing along her walls and probing at a spot she could only label as exquisitely sensitive. The physicality carried her along, past the obvious dissonance as Tahl fucked her ruthlessly.

Powerful, measured thrusts built her response and the slap of flesh on flesh resonated in her head. The dominance was clear, a different kind of connection, and one she feared would be her lot in life. One she'd brought upon herself.

His smooth motion losing rhythm, Tahl yanked her upright by dint of wrapping a hand around her hair. He held her against him, his pelvis moving choppily as his free hand sought her clit. Already sensitive, she hissed in protest, but he rubbed with enough pressure to draw yet another orgasm that left her clenching helplessly around his turgid cock.

With a growl, he came, heat washing her insides, and then he lowered her trembling body. She buried her face as he pulled out and dropped to his back. She felt the distance between them acutely, and cautiously straightened her legs to face away from him. Confused and saddened, she allowed one paltry tear to escape and slide over the bridge of her nose to dampen the pillow.

He twitched the sheet over her, but she didn't trust her voice enough to respond and felt him leave the bed. The sound of silence echoed as she closed herself off, knowing she'd made a horrible mistake.

****

Tahl turned the dial on the shower to the coldest setting and tolerated the spray for several minutes. It didn't help to numb the pain in his chest. Shifters didn't suffer from the maladies that plagued humans, at least not until they were much, much older than his thirty-one years, but he idly wondered if he was having a heart attack. More likely, he was suffering from a broken one.

With a mental huff, he turned off the water and stepped out to dry himself. What the hell was wrong with him that he kept pushing her? Sleeping in the same bed had sorely tested his self-control, and when she'd cuddled into him, murmuring against his neck, her leg thrown perilously close to his cock…

His wolf had raged, despising the barrier of the ugliest nightwear he'd ever seen as a man, drawn by her scent and proximity. Her heat no longer a factor, the animal should have been sated to a large degree but was as randy as ever.

She'd tried to retreat, but he'd followed, made his intentions clear, and while she hadn't refused him, her ambivalence had been clear. Rubbing at his hair, he tried not to think about how much it hurt when she rebuffed his attempt to kiss her. Only an idiot would have misinterpreted that message, though the label might not be misplaced where he was concerned.

So he'd taken her the way his wolf preferred, in a dominant, hugely satisfying manner, absolving her of implied intimacy. Tahl rubbed at that irritating soreness in his chest without making a dent in the discomfort. They'd both gotten off, but the act had been lacking somehow.

In the process of hanging up his towels, he froze. He knew how to fuck, had considerable experience at pleasuring any woman in his bed—or hers. He'd fucked his mate. Three times now, and found them to be immensely satisfying experiences, at least physically. But he hadn't made love to her, and perhaps never would.

Quietly stepping into a clean pair of boxers he drew from his dresser, he stared through the darkness at the huddled form of his mate, her sonorous breathing reaching his ears. He doubted she was asleep and was torn between crawling in beside her to hold her close, while risking another rebuff, or withdrawing. *He who fights and runs away lives to fight another day.*

His lips twitched with surprise. His wolf didn't subscribe to that notion, but perhaps his brain was stepping up and actually overruling both his animal and his cock. Making a brief stop in the guest bath and a hurried trip back to the ensuite, he headed to the small room he kept locked at all times. The space was where he kept his records and a wide assortment of weapons. Being mated, even newly mated didn't mean his responsibilities diminished, and he owed Jett another update this week. Outside of the Dawnfall pack, only Tahl, and his Alpha were aware of the danger that might still stalk his kind. He believed he'd eradicated the risk, but only time and considerable follow-up, would tell.

Not knowing which side of Desiree he would face in the morning would keep him on his mettle, and he regretted that he had to leave her so soon. Even for a day. That she would endeavor to continue to build space between them was a given. A hint of despair flickered in the back of his mind, but he ignored it. He needed to give it time and trust that the Desiree he so fondly remembered still lived inside the unhappy female he now cohabitated with.

Chapter Six

She'd lain awake until dawn after Tahl had left their bed, hearing him shower and wander to and fro. She'd wondered if he might return, telling herself that was something she didn't want. When early morning light crept around the edges of the blinds, she got up, a tired, sticky and sweaty mess.

The house was silent and she accepted he'd left for the day, ignoring the twinge she experienced at the idea. Best if he wasn't around, as even his presence chipped away at her resolve. Last night had been a monumental mistake. A few minutes of pleasure, okay, ecstasy, wasn't a fair trade-off for the self-doubt and recriminations afterward, not to mention feeling abandoned.

Ridiculous. She snatched up her cozy pajamas and clutched them to her chest as she marched down the hall. He might make her share his bed, but she was staking her claim on the main bathroom. Folding the nightwear and placing it on top of the hamper, she reached for her brush, blinking with surprise at the empty countertop. A quick glance through the vanity drawers confirmed all of her toiletries were missing, though her makeup was still there.

Turning on her heel, she made her way to the ensuite and glared. Her toothbrush and paste sat to the left of the sink, beside Tahl's, her brush on the opposite side beside a disreputable comb with missing teeth. Her lotions and potions were lined up neatly and she could see her shampoo and conditioner on the shelf in the shower.

Clenching her fists, she longed to sweep every last item onto the floor and hurl the hair products against the mirror.

"There's nothing sexier than a woman's things in my bathroom. Except maybe you in a rage."

Whirling, she glared at the shifter lounging in the doorway. She was getting her hearing checked damn soon. "You moved my stuff."

"I did."

"Goddamn it, Tahl," she began before becoming fully aware of her nudity. She'd dreaded the awkwardness she anticipated after last night, but this was beyond awkward.

"Are you cold?" He gestured at her chest, where her traitorous nipples beaded.

"I'm not cold. I'm pissed off."

He stepped forward, crowding her and she gave ground. He tugged the glass shower door open and leaned in to fiddle with the controls until a steaming patter of water filled the enclosure. "There're fresh towels, and I hung your scrubby thing on the tap."

Scrubby thing? She followed his gaze and took in her bath poof. Angry tears warred with an insane need to laugh. "You're a terrible, pushy roommate," she said. "Now go away."

"You don't need my help? Washing your back?"

"No!" She gestured toward the hall. "Go."

He brushed a kiss across her tangled hair. "I made coffee, but you'll have to tend to your own breakfast. I'm on my way to Jett's."

"Like that?" She'd pretended not to notice that he was clothed only in a pair of silky black boxers.

"Is that a hint of humor, Desi?"

At least he wasn't calling her baby, anymore. Stupid endearment. "No. Just an observation."

With a wink, he sauntered away and she slammed and locked the door—without taking notice of his fabulous ass. If he needed anything from in here before he left, too bad. She picked up the comb with two fingers and dropped it into the trash can. No wonder his hair always had that *just out of bed* look.

She stepped into the shower, taking comfort in the fact he'd forgotten her body wash, and used his spicy soap with abandon. If her skin dried up, served him right, although it wasn't like she was going to encourage any closeness for him to find out.

God, she was thinking like a girl. Or with her pussy. As she washed the evidence of their sex away, her fingers lingered as she recalled the way he'd lavished so much attention on her. Could she have regular ... sexual encounters with someone she didn't like and who she resented? And who wouldn't care for her at all anymore if the truth as she feared it came out? Her body and her wolf certainly didn't seem to mind, as long as she could forget how messed up it made her feel. Like she was playing with fire.

She wandered his home, wrapped in a towel, her hair turbaned in another, and carrying a perfectly prepared cup of coffee. He'd definitely left this time, a brief note on the table like a punch in the belly.

Desi- Home for dinner. I'll cook. Be safe. Tahl

It was the kind of missive her dad would leave for her mom, although it lacked the "love" before the signature. But then this wasn't a love match. The note underscored her current position in life and within the pack. Word would soon spread and she'd be subject to both speculative glances and curious questions. Some of the other females would be pissed, and she could do without the bitchiness.

Leaving the paper where she'd found it, she thought about the locked door down the hall. She was curious, but Tahl had a right to his secrets, just as she had a right to her own. Probably all mated pairs kept secrets, and it shouldn't bother her.

With a glance at the time, she hustled to apply her makeup and choose an outfit for the day. Opening the shop and working from Tahl's house didn't require anything fancy. Finding a pair of panties, she pulled out a pair of yoga pants and long-sleeved matching top. Her small, high breasts didn't require a bra, though her fingers lingered over the gossamer one he'd given her at the cabin, before consigning it to a pile of items to be washed. On an impulse, she slipped the silly pink thongs on her feet.

After running her brush through her damp hair, she carefully hung her towels to mimic Tahl's tidiness. A pang of some undefined emotion lanced through her at the thought of the room harboring other women's belongings, not that his past conquests bothered her anymore.

She drove to her mother's store and unlocked it, and then disarmed the security system. Everything looked the same as it did a couple of days ago, and she paused to straighten an artfully tied scarf on a mannequin. She sniffed at the air, marking the perfume her mom favored and wished she was here. Though she'd wished—fiercely—that people would leave her alone… It was a good thing she hadn't given that desire a voice or she might never see another soul. If a person really believed she was capable of such things.

Waiting on Michelle, she called River. Her friend was again unwell, and not up for a visit in any shape or form. Jett had hired a nanny so Desi wasn't even required to help out. She made a mental note to send the other woman a gift from the boutique—River had the fashion sense of a gnat, and wanted to dress appropriately as the Alpha's mate. Desi needed to keep in mind her sister-in-law's changing shape, and absently drifted a hand down to her belly.

How are you, little one? Forgive your mommy's silliness. She'll figure it out soon enough.

"Desi?" Michelle clattered in, the blonde shifter female the perfect advertisement for the boutique. Today she was wearing an outfit Desiree had coveted for herself. "Am I late?"

Michelle was always late, and often unavailable for reasons known only to herself, but once she arrived she remained a focused and efficient employee.

"You're good." She abruptly changed her mind. "I'll be working out of Marlene's office today as soon as I run a few errands." Like running back to Tahl's and grabbing her laptop.

"I'm fine alone," Michelle said. "Really. It's not like some weirdo's going to target a boutique."

"I'd feel better." She couldn't stay by herself at Tahl's.

"Whatever you like." The blonde was a bit huffy, perhaps thinking Desi didn't think she could manage. She narrowed her eyes. "Hey. Are you okay? You look different."

With a self-deprecating wave over her outfit, she said, "Casual Friday."

Michelle's mouth gaped at the sight of her flip flops. "I'll say. Though it's not just your clothes."

Tahl might be spreading the word by now, and if not him, then Jett. She didn't know if the Council was meeting today, but she didn't want to look as though she had a reason to hide anything. Better she brazen it out.

"Must be the glow," she joked.

"Glow? Yeah, maybe… Hey, are you pregnant? That kind of glow?" Michelle vibrated, her face speculative. "Are you mated?"

"Two days ago. Pregnant too." Shifters sometimes miscarried, but it didn't feel as though she was jinxing herself by telling Michelle. But it made it frighteningly real, and her mouth dried out.

"Wow. Who claimed you?"

"Tahl Powers."

A brittle smile etched Michelle's full lips although her face paled in shock. "I suppose I shouldn't be surprised. He's dogged your footsteps this past while. It's a good match, what with his position on the Council and you being the Alpha's sister."

Nothing about a grand passion or undying love. Desi fought the urge to laugh out loud. The other woman had summed it up succinctly. She smiled back, certain her effort was as transparent as Michelle's. Michelle, who was also approaching her twenty-fifth birthday.

Quietly, Desi said, "Well, he's off the market now."

"Right. Well, congratulations. All the best." Michelle turned to leave, probably already envisioning the first phone call she'd make, and then looked back. "Whatever happened with that female he went after over at Dawnfall?"

The dart found its mark, but Desi was ready for it. "Can't say."

"Well, with females earning the right to refuse before the male triggers her heat, she probably made use of it. I guess I'd be okay with being second choice, seeing as it's Tahl."

"Exactly." She faced the other woman down until Michelle finally left to enter her information into the till and throw on the Open sign.

Maybe it would be best to hide out at Tahl's after all. There would be a steady stream of the curious and the so-called well-wishers as soon as Michelle made that first call. Being forced to see all those shifters was daunting. Not to mention the humans, though they would think in terms of marriage because he'd knocked her up. Bleck. On the bright side, it would drive sales and she could always plead work demands to avoid any lengthy discussion.

Grabbing her purse, she waved to Michelle, cell glued to the other woman's ear. "I'll be back in an hour or so."

As she feared, there were a number of females in the shop when she returned with her laptop. She'd taken the time to change, not caring about what Michelle might think. A beautiful, pale-blue wool suit worn over a feminine shirt and four-inch stilettos gave her confidence.

A chorus of congratulations, followed by any number of questions ranging from the mundane to the sublime and unforgivably intrusive filled the air.

"How long have you two been an item?"

"When are you due?"

"When did this happen?"

"What's Tahl like as a mate?"

"He's amazing in the sack, Desi. Probably even better what with your heat, eh?"

She fielded all of them with a sweet smile and as little information as possible, saying it was one of those things and that he was probably like any other mate, seeing as she had no basis for comparison. As for the snide reminder that she got to share his sexual largesse with any number of others, she took a page out of Tahl's book and winked. Though it about killed her to remain above it all.

To her surprise, there were also sincere congratulations and kindness shown by some members of the pack, especially from those who drifted in later. Even a few of the females she knew had either been with Tahl or might have seen themselves in her place were in that category.

But toward the end of the work day, she was drained. She'd managed a little work and dealt with the parade of "customers". Michelle was also exhausted, though visibly pleased with her commission sales. The front door opened and Desi swallowed a groan. She hoped the straggler wouldn't draw things out.

Michelle's voice reached her. "Tahl! How nice to see you. I hear congratulations are in order."

His deep voice answered. "They are indeed. Thanks. Is Desi in the back?"

When the other woman replied in the affirmative, she heard him move quietly toward the office and somehow resisted smoothing her hair and checking her makeup. He'd seen her at her very worst and gilding the lily, as her nana would have said, was stupid.

"Desiree." He didn't sound pleased with her and she studied his handsome face. His very presence made her breath hitch.

"Hello, Tahl."

"I thought you were working at home today."

"I changed my mind." Intuiting an upcoming disagreement, she rose and went to squeeze past him. "See you tomorrow, Michelle."

"Okay. Bye, love birds!"

As soon as the other female was out of hearing, she said, "Have I broken another one of your edicts?"

"I expect that if I'd gone home and didn't find you there, I'd have been disappointed, seeing as you aren't where you said you'd be."

"Right. I forgot. You're my father now."

"What I'd like to do to you right now hardly falls into the paternal category, though you might think smacking your ass qualifies."

"What's wrong with you?"

"I think it's more about you."

She retreated behind the desk, wary of the tight reserve in his voice. "I'll be sure to update you regarding my itinerary from here on in."

"Jesus, Desi. I was in Council all morning, and there were some fires to put out afterward as a result of our discussions. River was inundated with calls because people couldn't reach Jett, and she's not feeling well."

"Tahl, I have no idea what you're talking about."

"You told a number of people that we're mated."

"So? Were you planning on hiding it?" She couldn't imagine that, but the very idea stabbed her right beneath her sternum.

With an exasperated sigh, he said, "Family is told initially, after the Alpha if permission hasn't been granted, a moot point, in this case, then the Council. Then the freaking pack at large. You know that. I was blindsided. And on top of that, you weren't answering your cell."

Keeping an eye on him, she fished through her purse, brow furrowing. "It's not here. I have no idea how I didn't notice. Crap, I hope I didn't lose it."

"Normally, the happy couple are presented to the Council. Often there's a party. But I suppose your take on our union is such that all of that is irrelevant."

With a sinking stomach, as she fully recognized his angst, she said, "I told Michelle because she noticed something different about me. I guess she spread the word."

"Like wildfire," he agreed, his tone as dry as the desert. "I imagine you had some visitors today."

"Pretty much all the females in the pack who could get away from their jobs. Several human females.

I'd estimate *all* of your conquests." She wasn't feeling badly enough to resist making that jab.

Silence weighed heavy in the small space, thick and suffocating. "And you thought you'd face each and every one of them on your own."

Tahl would know how other females reacted— and some of the males too—when a pair bond was formed. Jealousy resulting from disappointment wasn't uncommon. She'd seen it in River's case despite the fact that those mated were totally loyal to one another because there was no alternative.

She shrugged. "It was okay."

"Because it didn't touch you." His tone was weary, and his shoulders slumped.

"Tahl." She might not like him and was still so very angry that he'd triggered her heat, but she shouldn't hurt him. They had to make the best of this relationship. Yet she wasn't prepared to open herself up to him by telling him that every female he'd taken had been like a body blow for her over the years. "Your past is what it is. There's nothing changing it."

On a gust of breath, he said, "I was fucking jealous of your ... flirtations. I thought you were doing all those males, not that I had the right to feel that way."

She sat down before her knees buckled and kept her composure. "Well, now you know I wasn't doing any of them, you can stop questioning your rights."

"Why *did* you wait, Desi? Truth."

She shook her head. "It doesn't matter."

"Tell me. Truth."

Looking him straight in the eyes, she said, "I wanted my first time to be with someone I deserved, and who deserved me."

Wincing, he let out a bitter laugh. "I had to ask. I'll try to be that someone from here on out. Best I can do. I'll see you at home."

She stared after him, hearing the door shut quietly behind him, and wondered why there was such a weight on her chest. It finally lifted to allow her to take in enough air to banish the darkness around the edges of her vision, and she slowly packed up.

The landline rang and she stared at it as though it might turn into a snake. Could she deal with another pack member? Picking it up, she clicked the talk button.

"Desiree?" Her mother spoke before she could.

"Uh huh."

"You're not answering your cell."

"I left it somewhere."

"You're attached to that thing. This connection with Tahl must have addled your thinking."

"Gee, thanks, Mom."

"Michelle texted me. Several times. I called Lizbeth."

"Good, thanks." She should have called her sister, but that female was so blissed out in her relationship with Gareth that Desi couldn't have stood the shrieking excitement. Or the marked disparity.

"I should have stayed. Been a support. But this buying trip came up and… It's not something I could have rescheduled."

"No problem, Mom. It's not like you could have done anything more. I mean, you encouraged him."

"You're angry with me."

"And him." *And myself.*

"You've always wanted him. You haven't looked at anyone else seriously. I confess I'm ambivalent as usual. But I told him to tell you what was in his heart."

"He said he cared for me. Right before he triggered my heat. Maybe I'm okay as a second choice."

"It's more than that, honey."

"I jinxed him with Peyton, Mom."

Faint breathing crackled over the phone. "It's possible."

At least Marlene wasn't downplaying the possibility, but that was likely because of her own abilities. "I screwed up, being all hurt and angry. He was following his heart and I ruined it for him. And I ended up with someone who settled." She choked on a scalding burst of laughter. "Karma."

"Then you'll have to make the best of it."

"On it, Mom. Oh, and I'm pregnant so you get to be a grandmother again." She knew it irked Marlene to feel her age, though she loved Lizbeth and Gareth's pups to bits, not to mention River and Jett's.

"That's wonderful, Desi." Her mother's voice rang with sincerity.

"Yeah, well, I always wanted kids."

"You'll be a great mother. Just try not to follow my example too closely."

"I won't." At her mother's huff, she smiled. "Kidding. Uh, Mom? Do you ever have visions?"

"You know I do. What's this about?"

"I'm talking visions about someone you know. With you in them."

"No. Not like that. Why?"

"I think I had one, although it might just have been because I was so upset." That's what it was, she decided. "Probably my temper giving me fits."

"Could be," her mother said, caution evident in her tone. "What was it about?"

"Killing Tahl."

"Desiree!"

"I told you I was angry."

"Then that's probably what it was, a visual manifestation of your fury."

"Probably?" Maybe she should be concerned. It was one thing to jinx someone with a comment, quite another to act on one herself. She'd never…

With an exasperated sigh, Marlene said, "Pay attention, Desi. And call me if you have one again."

"The way he and I relate, I expect I'll experience several," she said drily.

"Honey, I'm sorry. Sometimes I wish I'd never met your father. Or Jett's."

"Well, you're on your own now, Mom. Are you happy?"

"Not especially. But I'm not getting involved again. And I'm not talking about that part of my life with my youngest daughter."

On a sigh, she said, "Sure. See you when I see you."

She set the cordless back in the charger and made herself get up and head out. She armed the system and locked the door, glad she'd at least talked to her mom on the phone, even if she hadn't eased her mind much. The Fae blood had manifested in different ways in all of Marlene's children, but Desi felt cursed.

Keeping it a secret wasn't easy, but her mother was afraid of someone using her as a weapon. Marlene wasn't inclined to write all of the events off as coincidences. She smiled now at the thought, a bitter grimace. Anyone who tried to force her to use her so-called ability would be treated to their own punishment.

True to his word, Tahl was at home and preparing their evening meal. With a wince, she recalled her promise to pick up groceries. In all the furor, she'd missed lunch too, and her coffee was a bare memory, so the smell of roasting chicken made her belly rumble.

"Smells great."

"Thanks. I put it in the oven a few minutes ago.

It'll be ready in an hour or so." He kept his distance, not that she expected anything else.

"I'll do the shopping tomorrow."

"Good." He headed down the hall and let himself into that locked room, so she retreated to the spare bedroom.

Changing back into her yoga pants and top, she again forewent a bra. Her phone had been in the console of her car, dead as a doornail, so she located her spare charger and plugged it in, doing the same with her laptop. Did making the best of it mean she should go out and clean up and set the table?

Reluctant to leave the relative sanctuary of the room, she sank down on the bed and studied her bare feet, making a mental note to schedule a mani-pedi. She was hopeless, and no doubt Tahl was busily regretting his impulsive act.

On a whim, she called River, her tethered phone seriously hampering her movements. Jett answered and advised her his mate was sleeping.

"How sick is she?" Surely when she'd wished for people to leave her alone, she hadn't visited this on her sister-in-law's head? It made her dizzy, knowing she couldn't police her thoughts. Watching her mouth was difficult enough.

"She's tired. The doctor was by and isn't concerned." Jett sounded frustrated. "Shifters aren't supposed to endure morning sickness. It's a rarity. But leave it to River to be different."

"How long has she been dealing with it?"

"Weeks."

So, not her then. The relief made her weak and she swayed, catching her balance against the dresser. Thinking it, wishing it, didn't make it happen. "But she'll be okay."

"She will." His voice was firm. "Uh, Desi? As Alpha I officially approve, as your brother, well, I'm sorry."

"For what? Following tradition?" Okay, she was still pissed at him.

"That, and assuming."

"Assuming?"

"That you're still ass over heels for Tahl. If I'm wrong I apologize, despite the fact he'll be good to you. I seriously couldn't have chosen a better male."

"I can't talk to you about this, Jett. I'm not sure I'll ever forgive you, either." She swallowed a sob and glanced at the closed door. With Tahl behind another such barrier, her privacy should be guaranteed, but she pressed the phone closer to her ear.

"Don't you cry, little sister. Just don't." He'd never been able to cope when she wept, probably because she did it so infrequently.

For the second time that day, she unveiled the elephant, although not in the same manner as with her mother. Though Jett would understand. It was simply that she didn't want anyone else to know what she might be capable of. They'd run far and fast.

Nearly whispering, she said, "He wanted Peyton. And for whatever reason, settled for me. It's a hard pill to swallow, and I'm gonna need a whole lot of time to adjust, if ever. If you know of a way of breaking a mated bond, now's the time to throw out that secret."

"Desi, I want you to listen to me. I'm not going to elaborate, so don't ask, but you listen. Tahl was fooled. He didn't actually want Peyton Leaf. And he didn't settle for you. He counted himself fortunate that you hadn't made a commitment to another male when he returned. Fucking fortunate."

She opened her mouth to probe and then closed it

again. There was a mystery there, but Jett wasn't going to share it. She recognized that tone. "Okay."

"You don't believe me. You don't believe Tahl. Are you planning to let your pride fuck up what could be a great connection? Like what River and I have? Lizbeth and Gareth?"

"It's not only my pride," she said.

"What does that mean?"

"There's some things I can't tell you either, big brother." *Like the terror of failing to guard my mouth adequately where you and yours are concerned these past few years and inadvertently changing your future.*

"Desi."

"Sorry. Gotta go. My love to River and the kids." She hardly felt childish at all, in not including him in the good wishes.

Chapter Seven

Another shared meal interspersed with awkward silences, and Desi wondered if it was incumbent on her to make the first move.

"I'll have to make a doctor's appointment in a couple of weeks or so."

The knife he was using to efficiently slice through a piece of dark meat paused infinitesimally before it lightly scraped the plate. Tahl fixed his gaze on hers. "Probably a good idea."

Unable to read him, she nodded and went back to pushing food around. It seemed they were slated to meet only at mealtimes—and in his bed. Saddened, but unable to see her way clear, she let the silence roll out.

When he stood to clear their plates, she took the opportunity to hurriedly put away everything else, busy work, and then escaped to her makeshift office with a mumbled excuse. Her cell was vibrating and she grabbed for it as though it was a lifeline.

"Desi?"

River. "Hey. How are you?"

"Over whatever it was, I think. This is the last pup."

"Really?"

"Really. Three is enough unless this pregnancy goes significantly easier for the remainder of my term."

They discussed being pregnant, and raising children for a few minutes, with Desi steadfastly steering the conversation away from labor and delivery. Her left hand kept straying to her belly and she finally allowed it to rest there in a silent blessing.

"How's it going with Tahl?"

"It's going." *Nowhere.*

"Are you … sleeping with him?"

Buying time, she teased, "River. Are we going to share dirty details?"

"No! I'm sorry. I thought… It's just that I remember how you talked about exploring your … fantasies, and all. I guess I hoped you might find a middle ground with him."

She had blithered on to River about precisely that thing, way back when, and hectic color heated her face. She avoided the question. "I don't want to."

"Uh, you don't want to tell me? Or—"

"I don't want to sleep with him."

"Oh. Well, okay, I guess. You won't have to for a long time, seeing as you're pregnant. But I guess I'm worried. Jett said you were really unhappy. And that you hate him."

"I feel betrayed, River. My own brother and his damn tradition. Shifter destiny. I don't hate him. I just need some time."

"Well, don't be a stranger, okay?"

"I won't," she promised.

Flopping on the bed, she stared at the ceiling. Maybe River was right. If she had to share space with Tahl, she might as well—what was she thinking? Might as well tie her life up in a nice little package and risk having it shredded, like her heart.

With a sigh, she rolled to a seated position. She didn't feel like working, was in fact caught up, and it wasn't like she'd be able to concentrate. Reaching for her ereader, she tapped through until she found a suspenseful romance. The words blurred and she set the device aside in exasperation.

Normally, at home, she'd watch a little television. Tahl must be in that locked room—she'd come to the conclusion it was his office, so now they both had a place to hide out in. Well, *she* was hiding. Tahl was likely doing whatever her brother's lieutenant did for the pack. Grimacing at her flippancy, she accepted that he was indeed Jett's right-hand man, respected and an asset.

She flinched, remembering his disappointment regarding her premature announcement of their affiliation. Her mother should be organizing a party like she'd done for Jett and River once her sister-in-law had recovered from the rogue shifter attack. And after Jett pulled his head out of his ass regarding his true feelings for River.

Desi didn't want a party, although it would go a long way to smoothing ruffled feathers and ease Tahl's obvious pain. Not that she cared if he was hurting. Except she did. She had to make the best of this and an armed détente wasn't the best plan after all.

Considering her passionate outbursts, she twisted her lips in a rueful grimace. Setting aside her pride—and her anxiety—for the time being, she went in search of her mate. She scanned the living area and passed through the kitchen, ending up in front of the slightly ajar door of his office.

In truth, she'd followed her ears. Tahl was speaking in low tones and in getting closer, she understood he was talking about her. Or at least, their relationship.

"We'll present a united front to the pack, Alpha. Desi isn't stupid, regardless of how she feels about me. She is fully aware of keeping up appearances." A pause, and then, "I have no idea what else precludes her from giving me a chance. None. But then we aren't talking. We're either painfully polite or arguing."

At least he didn't tell her brother he'd managed to seduce her or tout their sexual connection. Having heard enough, she rapped sharply on the wooden panel.

"Gotta go."

She heard a chair creak and his quiet footsteps, so forced a smile on her face as the door opened.

"Hey." He looked tired, faint circles beneath his emerald eyes and strain etched around his mouth. Her palm itched with the need to rest on his cheek, maybe soothe those fine lines with her fingertips.

He didn't invite her into his domain, blocking the door with his bulk, so she retreated to rest her back against the wall. "Marlene won't be home for a while, so I thought we might organize a party."

His stare didn't waver, though she looked for any softening there. "We could do that."

Well, she didn't expect him to jump up and down, but hoped for a bit of enthusiasm, seeing as she was offering an olive branch. "Only if you want."

"Why don't you and River figure out a venue, make up an invitation list—"

"Sure." She didn't care if he didn't. "I'll get on it."

"Desi." She kept walking. "Desi."

"It's fine, Tahl. Go back to what you were doing," she called over her shoulder.

The door shut quietly, and she told herself it was his loss. At least she'd made the effort and now it was back to being a good roommate.

Snagging the laundry hamper, she sorted their clothes, and sorted the whites from the darks, all the while concentrating on the task at hand. Starting a load, she hauled one of her boxes up onto the table and flipped open the lid.

She took her time situating her things, careful not to move anything of Tahl's, standing back to view the placement with a critical eye. Switching out the clothes into the dryer and shoving the rest into the washer, she worked quietly to empty the rest of the boxes.

The only place she didn't put anything was Tahl's bedroom. Common space was one thing, but she was loath to put her stamp on such a personal place.

Breaking down the boxes, she set them on the back porch, and checked for the recycling day, consulting the chart on the fridge. She retrieved the items from the dryer and folded them while the remaining clothes dried. The tasks were comfortingly familiar, although gave her too much time to think.

Her thoughts whirled and coalesced, but she came up with the same conclusion, over and over. Tahl could never find out she'd ruined his chance at happiness and a true mate and she'd have to carry on as best she could. She retained enough of her pride to decide to withhold her heart at all costs. She didn't trust him with it, in any event.

****

Listening to the faint sounds as Desi moved around the house, Tahl finally gave up on perusing the latest information coming out on the illicit drugs targeting the shifter population. The outbreak appeared to be contained, but his Alpha had tasked him with monitoring it. Tucking the files away, he locked the desk drawer, debating how he should proceed with Desiree.

He knew he'd fucked up with his indifferent response when Desi raised the party issue, but he hadn't been able to get past the obvious separation she'd established by prematurely sharing their union. It made a mockery of everything he'd hoped for. Scoffing, he accepted his own actions had brought most of it down on his head.

He'd also been puzzled by Jett's comment, his Alpha reaching out in a phone call. What was Desiree hiding, something as equally potent as her pride, that it would stand in the way of her making a concentrated effort in their union? Whatever it was, he doubted she'd share it, at least not anytime soon.

The walls closed in and he felt his office was more a cell than a place of work. He moved to the window and winched the blinds upward, looking out into the night. Nothing moved, the relatively tranquil back yard barely visible in the discreet lighting. He'd installed motion detectors to supplement the security system in the house, something especially important now he had a mate to protect as well as his unborn child.

He'd talk with her about the doctor visits, he decided. Plan to attend each and every one. If they could connect over anything, and enhance their pair bond, it would be over the pup. His wolf rolled over and made another suggestion, and despite his earlier despair, he couldn't disagree. The physical need for Desi simmered and he knew she wasn't immune to the same draw.

Exiting the office, locking up behind him, he paced down the hall, sniffing the fresh scents of laundry soap and bleach. One light burned dimly in the direction of the living area and he strode toward it, casting a glance into the master bedroom. It lay in darkness, but he made out the shrouded form of his mate curled up on the bed.

He continued to the kitchen and drew a glass of water from the tap, drinking it down. The clock in the other room ticked over, and the house settled, as if for the night. Girding his mental loins, he set the glass in the sink and headed for bed, clicking off the lamp Desi had left on for him. The little gesture was reassuring, and it reminded him of the female he'd grown up around.

It was doubtful she was asleep. Her body screamed tension, and he longed for the day when she'd be relaxed in his bed. Their bed. He'd purchased the colossal king upon his return from Dawnfall, sleeping alone each and every night for what felt like an eternity as she avoided him.

Stripping off, he tossed his clothes over a convenient chair and slid beneath the covers. There was an acre of space between them, something he resolved to deal with, both literally and figuratively. Starting now. He rolled over and dropped an arm around her waist. She stiffened but didn't demur.

"We'll talk about the party in the morning, baby." He tucked her up against him, his body instantly hardening. The silky stuff of the gown she wore slipped erotically against his heated skin.

"Sure." Her muffled response was hardly wholehearted, but at least she answered.

Splaying a hand over her hip, he stroked the curved flesh gently, his rough skin prickling over her nightwear. He allowed his breath to stir through her hair, making no attempt to hide his throbbing erection. It took a long time for her to relax, and then only to lift into his touch.

Her fragrant arousal signaled, and he eased away, drawing her along with him to sprawl on her back. Planting a knee on either side of her, he tugged her nightgown up, pleased that she facilitated his efforts, and drew it over her head. Even in the near dark, her long, slender form gleamed and his breath caught.

Abandoning all sense of additional foreplay, he lowered his weight. His desperate cock found its path unerringly to her gate, and he pressed home with one smooth thrust. Air gusted from their lungs with equal ferocity, and Tahl reveled in the hot, wet slickness gripping him. Biting back a groan, he dared to kiss her, but she turned her head to the side and his lips pressed against her cheek.

Accepting the boundary, though his beleaguered heart winced, he wrapped her up and held her tightly. They rocked together, as he desperately strove to convey the intimacy of the moment. Her palms pressed against his shoulders, alternately pushing him away and drawing him close.

Somehow, her ambivalence gave him the restraint he needed to make it good for her. Swiveling his hips on every upstroke, he worked the head of his cock deep until her smooth rhythm faltered and her breathing hastened. When the walls of her channel began to tighten and flutter, he thrust harder, pushing her over.

A muffled shriek passed her lips and she sobbed against his skin. He let himself follow, buttocks clenching as he filled her with his seed in a climax that blurred his vision. "I love you, Desi."

The only sign that she'd heard was a sharp intake of breath, and he waited in vain for any verbal response. He'd put it out there and had to trust she wouldn't use it against him, although there was a part that regretted making himself so vulnerable.

Easing out of her, he marked the rush of their combined juices, taking comfort in the fact they had chemistry in their favor. Deciding not to clean up, reveling in the evidence of their physical connection, he positioned himself beside her. When she didn't roll onto her side and give him her back, his chest lifted on a flicker of hope. Resting a possessive hand on her thigh, he gave over to sleep.

*****

I love you, Desi. Stunned didn't begin to cover it. After that involuntary intake of air, her vocal cords froze solid and her body felt disconnected from her brain—or controlled by her complacent wolf. How could he love her? He'd loped off into the distance all the way to the

Dawnfall pack after that Alpha's granddaughter. A shifter didn't leave the one he loved behind.

Everything felt into chaos, any ordered thoughts swept aside, while Tahl slumbered peacefully beside her, their skin touching at shoulder and hip, his big hand lying heavily on her thigh.

Her body cooled though her mind was heated. Carefully, she shifted away, Tahl's fingers slipping to trail to the bed, an involuntary shiver overtaking her. The firm mattress barely compressed as she swung her weight to the edge and set her feet on the floor. Her nightgown was a drift of fabric beneath her toes, and she leaned to scoop it up and drop it over her head. She instantly felt less exposed—physically. The garment did nothing to block her raw emotions.

Making her way down the hall, she shut herself in the main bathroom, flicking on the light but avoiding her reflection in the mirror. His proclamation was made in the aftermath of an orgasm, she decided. Sex made it easy to misinterpret many things, like one's feelings, saying words a person didn't really mean in the cold light of day—or so she'd heard.

With a shaking hand, she turned on the faucet and grabbed a cloth to clean herself up, the warm water easing her a trifle. She'd pretend she hadn't heard him, and hope he didn't repeat himself because at some point she'd reciprocate and then they'd be living an even more awkward, unbalanced lie.

Drying off, she tossed the cloth into the hamper and returned to his room on little cat feet, praying he didn't wake. Tomorrow would be soon enough to face him, to cobble together some kind of front to present to him. He snored lightly, and she felt his presence intensely, her heart hammering behind the prison of her ribcage.

She slid into her space and curled up, her back to him, not even bothering to pull up the covers. *I love you, Desi.* Had she *said* something to make that true? False? Not for the first time, she cursed her so-called ability—and her inability to always watch her mouth. She was calling Marlene first thing.

Chapter Eight

Desi slept, her hands tucked beneath the pillow, cradling her head. Knees raised toward her chest, the curve of her back and high roundness of her hip painted a sweet picture. Her long, black hair partially covered her face, tendrils quivering before the onslaught of her steady breaths. Tahl's heart ached. Finally, his, if not willingly. His wolf huffed, hardly caring about semantics, only nature.

Determined not to reflect on past circumstances, he made his morning ablutions as quietly as possible, returning to the bedroom to find her gone. The enticing smell of brewing coffee suggested her current whereabouts and he hustled to his dresser. Pulling out a drawer, he stilled. Normally a tidy person, he tended to pile in his socks and boxers, a non-issue seeing as they were all identical and there was no need to sort his socks.

Everything was neatly folded and placed in piles, like with like, and the clean fragrance of softener wafted to his nostrils. He patted one such pile in an absurd gesture, affected by the evidence of a feminine touch. Pulling his clothes on, he strode to the kitchen.

Desi gave him a faint smile, looking everywhere but at him. "Coffee's on. I have to go in early to the shop. Michelle texted me that she's sick."

Shifters essentially enjoyed good health, so Tahl doubted Michelle's excuse if she'd even made it. Was Desi running again? "I'll put some breakfast together while you get ready."

"I'm not hungry, thanks."

"You need to eat, Desi. Take care of yourself."

"I do. I'll get something delivered." She hurried away, swathed in the silky fabric that did little to disguise her feminine curves.

Realizing she'd been up in the night, in order to put her nightgown back on, Tahl frowned. He'd probably spooked her, chased her away with his spontaneous avowal of love. The woman turned him inside out and wrenched away his control. He was never fucking spontaneous, always thinking, considering. Yet he didn't regret his honesty.

Crossing to the fridge, he took out some fruit, quickly washing it and placing it in a bag. Checking the expiry date, he added a container of yogurt. He hesitated and then found the bread and peanut butter. Desiree loved the sticky spread, and he built her a sandwich, cutting off the crusts and wrapping it up in plastic wrap.

He was cooking eggs when she emerged, looking gorgeous in one of those tight skirts and a sexy top. He longed to free that mane of hair, to let it spill over her shoulders and down her back, but conceded she looked professional with it upswept. Despite her smile, he detected the strain behind it.

"I made you some breakfast, and a go-cup."

"Oh. Thank you." She drew her purse strap higher to slip the sack over her wrist and clutched the cup in her other hand alongside her keys.

"Any idea what time you'll be home?"

"After closing. But I need to pick up groceries."

He nearly offered to take on that chore but sensed she felt a real need to contribute. "I'll watch for you, help you carry them in."

"Sure." She sketched an awkward wave and inched toward the exit.

He matched her pace and then closed the distance, opening the door for her. Taking advantage of her having her hands full, he grasped her shoulders to tug her close and pressed a kiss on her forehead. "See you tonight. We'll talk about the party over dinner."

With a startled look, she nodded and tapped toward her car on those amazing shoes. He stood like a statue, watching her sexy stride, wrestling with the desire to haul her back in the house and to the bedroom where he'd keep her occupied for the next several hours.

Returning to his eggs, now cooked solid to a rubbery texture, he scraped them into the trash. He threw together another sandwich and grabbed his go-cup. Jett had an emissary coming from a far-flung pack in Canada, and his place was at his Alpha's shoulder.

River again greeted him at the door, looking considerably better than the day before. Once upon a time he'd simply disarmed the system and walked inside, but that changed after the rogue attack. Now, everyone was scrutinized by security cameras and only then allowed admittance.

His Alpha's mate smiled. "Morning. Jett's in the study."

He touched her forearm. "You doing okay?"

"I am, thanks. You?"

"Good."

"Oh, that's good." She smoothed down the front of her shirt and avoided his gaze. "How's Desi?"

"She's fine. Had to go into the shop."

"I know. She texted me. It's a good thing Marlene can count on her, seeing as Michelle isn't always reliable."

He'd admit to a wave of relief that his mate hadn't lied to him in order to flee. "She's a hard worker."

"She always has been, despite how others sometimes perceive her."

He'd been one of them, he knew. Chastising Desi on the amount of money she spent, when it hadn't been any of his business. Except back then he'd felt as though it was. "I know her pretty well, River. Though I guess I saw what I wanted to see, sometimes."

"But things are going okay?"

"We're finding our way. Not exactly an auspicious start, but I care about her and I'll do right by her."

"I believe you." Hesitating, as though she wanted to say something else but thought better of it, she gestured for him to pass. "I'm to entertain the emissary's mate, so I'd better get a few things ready."

"River?"

"Yes?"

"Desi told Jett it was more than her pride getting in our way."

"He told me that too." She chewed on her bottom lip. "I ... I called her last night to see if I could help, but it went nowhere. I feel like I'm betraying her, even talking to you about it, but it freaked Jett, so I'm bothered too."

"She's stubborn. I doubt she'll tell me."

"Maybe we should ask Marlene."

He hadn't thought of that. Did women confide in their mothers? Especially when it involved rejection? Some might, but he doubted Desi would. "Better you ask her."

"I will. As soon as she returns."

"It might put a strain on your relationship, River."

"It might. But then Marlene and I struggle some anyhow. I think it's worth it because I'm worried about my friend."

"Thanks."

"I didn't say I'd share it with you."

He had to accept that. Jett would insist he be advised if it was relevant. He trusted his Alpha and his Alpha trusted his mate.

Jett was ensconced behind his desk, clicking through something on his laptop. Tahl preferred paper if he had to pore over anything, and said as much.

With a grunt, his Alpha replied, "I don't have enough storage room as it is. Just going over the documents the Alpha of Wide Sky sent over. Pretty straightforward as an alliance goes. They're asking that we house a few of their younger members and are willing to reciprocate."

"What? Like an exchange kind of thing?"

"Right. I suspect their isolation is proving to be an issue when it comes to mating."

"Not such a bad idea," Tahl allowed.

"It's not. We have all those females we absorbed after rescuing them from the rogues. I'm thinking some of them might be interested in moving. Especially the ones who aren't fitting in as well here as they'd hoped. River mentioned they feel like everyone here knows their story, and it stands to reason if they move to Wide Sky, there won't be that history. They can share what they want to."

"It could work."

Jett swiveled away from the computer and stood. "They'll be here shortly. Anything new with my sister?"

"Nothing. If I push her on her comment to you, I expect she'll feel ganged up on."

"You're right. I've already betrayed her, in her eyes, so hopefully she'll share in time."

He doubted it somehow, a deep intuition, but shrugged. "River is going to ask your mother."

Jett laughed. "Marlene is more likely to tell my mate than me. I get to thinking I know women, then I'm proven wrong."

Dismissing the mystery of Desiree, they went to meet the emissary of Wide Sky. Tahl wondered why the

Alpha hadn't made the trip, quickly asking Jett.

"Something to do with being refused entrance at the border. And something we'll need to nail down with his representative. Because we're not going down the same path as Dawnfall."

"It's hardly the same thing, Alpha. Hell, Ashton didn't understand the full extent."

"But he wasn't totally forthcoming. There are pack secrets and then there are dangerous secrets, Tahl. I'm done with those. You took care of it, but we might not get so lucky next time."

There wasn't time for further discussion, as his Alpha strode forward to open the door. Only one guard was present, to complement the emissary's protection, and Benjamin lounged close by. Appearances were deceiving. He could leap into action as fast—or faster—than even Jett. Recently coming of age, and with brains as well as brawn, Benjamin was on the fast track toward joining the Council.

A tall, spare shifter offered his hand and Jett took it. "Welcome to Blue Star."

****

It had been a long, boring day for the most part. Desiree wasn't inundated with customers, which should have given her lots of time to connect with her mother, but Marlene wasn't available. Or wasn't answering her phone on purpose.

With too much time on her hands, she fretted. And fretted some more.

The product held no interest for her, though she straightened the racks and dusted the displays. She did her best to focus and nearly fell on the occasional woman who popped in to browse, likely driving them away with her desperation.

By the end of the day, she was exhausted from

doing pretty much nothing. And she had yet to face Tahl. She closed up and headed for her favorite market, shopping with care, burning daylight. She hadn't let herself think about the sex preceding Tahl's assertion, though vignettes flitted through her consciousness all day.

It had had nothing of the urgency of the other times, felt sweeter, more intimate, and far more dangerous. She needed to keep such a connection at arm's length from here on out. Resolved, she paid for her purchases and loaded them into the car.

Driving home, her belly tightened and she forced herself to relax. Tahl would never find out about her ability and she could still guard her heart. She wouldn't stomp on his or use any softer feelings against him. She wouldn't.

True to his word, Tahl came out to the vehicle and helped carry in the bags. His tall figure now sported faded jeans that he filled out admirably, and she kept her looks to herself. Together they put the purchases away.

"How were things at the shop?" He gently took a heavy sack from her.

"Quiet." She cast around for something else to say. "How was your day?"

"Eventful. We met with the emissary from Wide Sky. We're forging an alliance."

"That's great." She meant it. In her mind, the more the packs connected, the better it was for shifters overall. They'd fragmented in the past with factions arguing over territory, and the best way to interact with humans. Many shifters avoided them all together, but with the population explosion and secular groups being regarded with suspicion, even those packs were forced to assume an acceptable front.

Tahl lifted a shoulder. "We're seen as a

progressive pack, and we attract the clans with more than their share of younger shifters."

Chatting desultorily about the pros and cons of being perceived as progressive, they made short work of the task.

"I ordered pizza, Desi. Is that okay?"

"What kind?"

"Half bacon, pepperoni and fresh mushroom, half cheeseburger. Okay?"

Her belly fluttered. Her favorites. "Sounds good. I'll go change."

The heat of his stare followed her as she headed for her room. Her office slash dressing room. Her winter clothes took up half the space in his closet, and the spare room was jammed full. Tahl always looked good, and he owed his fair share of clothing, so she could probably purge a little.

Slipping into some comfortable yoga pants and a loose t-shirt—pizza tended to require a little more room—she took a deep breath. Maybe the evening wouldn't be such a trial.

He scanned her from head to toe and her wolf stretched onto its toes, obviously not getting the message that her heat was assuaged and a child growing as a result. She made herself move casually into the living room, and chose a chair opposite from where Tahl sat on the couch.

"Have you given any thought as to when you want to have our announcement party?"

Lacing her fingers together, she said, "Depends on where you want to hold it."

"Not here. Not enough room."

The idea of the entire pack descending on them was beyond daunting.

"Desiree, I'll be there."

He'd read her mind—or more likely, her body language. "Right. It'll be fine."

"It will. You faced down the majority of the females."

He was teasing, and surprisingly the reminder of his conquests didn't bite as hard. It was in the past… She brought herself up hard. Past or not, things gone by had a nasty habit of surfacing. With a forced smile, she said, "We can't ask Jett and River to offer their home. Not with the kids."

"True enough. They were out with the nanny today and the house still felt full. And her sister, Cassie, is coming to stay for a while."

"Maybe we could rent someplace, have it catered…"

"I vote we issue a blanket invitation like Marlene did for River and Jett. People tend to get offended if left out, even inadvertently."

She knew Tahl could identify each and every pack member without effort. At least they didn't have to ask the leaders of other packs. Only alphas followed that tradition. "All right. I'll find a venue."

The doorbell rang and he was up on his feet in one smooth movement. He checked outside. "Pizza." Turning, he said, "Remember to keep the system armed, Desi, okay?"

He was likely a bit paranoid, but she knew how protective male shifters were. "Okay."

As he paid the driver, she fetched paper towels and plates from the kitchen, adding some parmesan cheese and chilies. The red wine beckoned, but of course, she couldn't drink so filled a pitcher with water and ice cubes.

Tahl dumped the box on the coffee table and went to the fridge to pull out a beer. "I sometimes eat in the living room."

"Sure." She and her mom rarely ate at the table unless they had company.

It was far from the awkward experience of the previous evening and she cautiously let herself enjoy the affable atmosphere. Tahl didn't even turn the television on to some sports channel, though Desi liked football. And rugby.

In the next moment, she wished he'd been distracted.

"Can we talk about us, Desi?"

"I thought we were." The thin crust turned to cardboard on her tongue.

Wiping his mouth, he took a swig of beer. Was he searching for courage or buying time? She schooled her features.

"You talked with Jett last night—"

"And he blabbed to you. God, and women get a rap for gossiping." She crumpled her napkin on her plate and made to rise.

"Desi. He's our Alpha and as such—"

"Maybe we should video our sex too. Let him critique it." She stood and carried her plate to the kitchen, shaking the detritus into the trash before clattering the china in the sink.

He followed her, standing too close for comfort. When he set a hand on her arm, she shook him off. "Don't."

"It's twofold, baby. He's your brother too. He's concerned, as is River. I can't tell you how I feel."

"Then, don't," she said, infusing her tone with sweetness. "We're mated, I've accepted it and yet you keep pushing." Okay, maybe not so sweet. "What is it you want from me?"

"Honesty. A confidence. Let me in so I can be

there for you as your mate."

It hovered on the very tip of her tongue, a ridiculous urge to blurt it out. *Hey, Tahl. I can influence a person's future simply by giving voice to it. And look! You got what you deserved. It didn't work out with Peyton because of me and see who you ended up with!* Uh, no. He'd come to believe her, because of who her mother was, and hate her for his loss and his resulting gain.

She might not have wanted this mating, but she couldn't face him, day after day, seeing his anger and disgust, let alone the impact on their children. Pressing a hand against her lower belly, she sent a fervent, soothing message to the baby, promising her child she'd do anything to ensure its safety. Male shifters were protective, but nothing compared to a female when it came to her pups.

Glancing at Tahl, his chiseled lips set in a straight line, she knew he wasn't going to give it up. She lifted a hand to ward him off, and nearly screamed at the blood staining it. Her head swam and she reeled. He was there in a heartbeat, drawing her into his arms, hard against his chest where his steady heartbeat grounded her.

"What's wrong? Is it the baby?" He half carried her to the couch and sat with her on his lap.

Waiting for her breathing to steady, she shook her head, drumming up something that wouldn't involve the truth of what she saw. "I got a bit lightheaded."

"Fuck. I'm sorry. I keep upsetting you. I'll quit, Desi. I'm being selfish, wanting everything right fucking now." He stroked her hair and tucked her closer. "I've had a long time to envision this and you're just catching up."

She'd never catch up. He loved her and envisioned *this*… Her heart ached. It was all false, built on Fae magic. A sob wracked her body and she fought against tears. On top of everything, he didn't need to comfort her.

With a massive effort, she said in a credibly calm voice, "I'm okay now. And I appreciate you not pushing anymore."

"You need time," he agreed. "Just know I'm here for you. Please, baby?"

"I know."

He helped her to her feet when she set a hand against his chest, and she managed a controlled walk back to her chair. He frowned at the distance but said nothing.

"Is there football?" she asked.

****

With Desi making an early night of it, Tahl slumped back on the couch, swinging his feet up to stretch out. She'd fixated on the game, calling out critiques of the plays the way she used to when he watched football at Jett's, growing up. To a casual observer, nothing seemed awry, but he was far from casual, especially when it came to his mate.

What in hell had happened? The first thing that leaped to mind was something happening with their child, and he cursed himself again for stressing her. Though she seemed in a constant state of agitation with whatever it was weighing on her mind. But her pallor, and the stark fear in her eyes, as well as the fine trembling of her entire body spoke to something equally as bad, or close to it.

He desperately wanted to get to the bottom of it and share the burden. Whatever it was, surely sharing it would ease her. Calling his Alpha would only worry him and his mate, although he'd likely share her reaction with Jett the next day. He hoped River had reached Marlene.

Securing his home, he walked the perimeter, a vague, intangible worry gnawing at his gut. When he stripped for bed, she stirred and drew the covers higher. Climbing in, he debated between giving her space or encroaching on it. His need to comfort her pushed him closer and he held her in a loose embrace. Sex was the furthest thing from his mind. "It'll be okay, baby."

Chapter Nine

"Mom, you need to call me right fucking now. I need you." Where was she? Desi tossed her phone on the desk. Marlene wasn't anywhere she said she'd be and hadn't answered anyone's call. Jett had already sent out a message to the pack in that area and would ask for local law enforcement support soon.

She'd gotten through the past few days on limited sleep, her nerves stretched to the limit, doing her job and her mother's. True to his word, Tahl hadn't pushed, but she caught him watching her, speculating, and could only hope he didn't reconsider.

Acting normal and pretending to settle into her new role was wearing, although now she couldn't drum up such outrage and indignation against poor, misguided Tahl, adjusting as his mate was marginally easier. They lived together quite easily, better than her and her mom.

He didn't initiate sex, seemingly content to merely hold her at night until he fell asleep. His interest was apparent in his jutting erection, but he didn't make a move to address it. And she told herself it was for the best, that she didn't need it either.

Perhaps being taken out of her head by some mind-blowing orgasms would feel great in the moment, but she'd never initiate it. Her guilt weighed too heavily.

Her cell dinged and she snatched it up. Finally. "Mom? Where are you?"

Sounding weary, Marlene said, "Out of cell coverage, honey. I'm sorry to worry you."

"What's going on?" She got up and went to push the door closed. Michelle was with a customer but tended to eavesdrop.

"I don't want to get into it over the phone, but I

think I found someone with some understanding of the Fae."

Air whooshed out of her lungs and she propped a hip on the desk. Jett had taken a careful look around for other Fae, but keeping Marlene's abilities under wraps was paramount. Enough shifters knew she wasn't human as it was, although it had never been a problem. Their Alpha owed a lot of his ability to rule at such a young age to his genetic inheritance. Brilliant was the best way to describe him when it came to governing. He hadn't been cursed like her…

"Who is it?"

"I'll tell you when I get home." Her mother's tone was laced with caution, making Desi's intuition prick. "Now you tell me what provoked that phone message."

"Another vision, well, the same one," she whispered. "I was upset with him again."

"Do you think you're going to kill your mate?" Marlene's voice held nothing but interest, and Desi wanted to scream.

"No! I mean, he makes me nuts, but once I accepted the inevitable I calmed down. Some."

"Really."

Sighing, she said, "He said he loves me. What am I supposed to do with that?"

"Finally."

"What?"

Her mother laughed. "I told him to tell you what was in his heart."

"What he *thinks* is in his heart. He loves Peyton."

"Maybe."

"Mom. Please." Unbidden, tears sprang to her eyes. She wanted her mother to fix things.

"It's only true if he didn't love you before he met

her."

"He didn't." *Or he wouldn't have left.*

"Ask him."

"I can't."

"Why not?"

Hope unfurled in her chest and clumsily stitched together her heart. Could she ask him, take that risk? And if he had feelings for her before, as her mother seemed to think, there might be an explanation. But if it wasn't the case... He wouldn't necessarily have to know what she'd done, but she'd know for sure instead of suspecting, and it would torture her even worse. Damn her mother for giving her the wrong answer.

"I don't want to know."

"Right. Then you need to think on it some more." Ever practical, that was her mom.

"What about the vision?"

"I don't know." Gravity weighed in Marlene's voice. "I doubt it's true, at least the way you think it is because you still love Tahl and it sounds like you don't hate him anymore."

She didn't. Maybe she never had, merely hid behind antipathy to survive. One thing she felt was that if something happened to him, she wouldn't want to continue. "If it's true I'll follow him."

"Don't be stupid. Drama used to be your middle name. I thought you'd outgrown it."

Her mother's harsh words like a cold splash of water in her face, she replied, "Tahl makes me regress."

"Think of what you saw as a warning. If it happens, it won't be such a shock." With that sage advice, Marlene's voice faded and the call dropped.

In turn, Desi dropped her head in her hands, trying to pull herself together. She'd need a padded cell if this kept up. Dialing Jett, she informed him their parent was alive and well and might have met another Fae. Or at least someone with knowledge. He was as incredulous as she and urged her to let Lizbeth know.

"When is she back?" he asked.

"The call dropped before I established that, but I think she's on her way."

"Contact me if you hear from her again," he ordered. "Our mother never ceases to amaze me. Buying trip. Right."

Maybe Marlene had one of her visions or something. Desi hoped it hadn't been generated because of her union with Tahl. Or maybe it was a good thing. Hell, she had no idea and her brain was turning to mush.

"Desiree?" Michelle rapped on the door.

Setting her questions and issues aside, she went to help the other woman with an ordering issue, seeing as the customer was so thin she required a size yet unknown to shifter or humankind.

The flowing red waves seemed familiar, but it took a second glance to confirm the other shifter's identity. Always slim, Peyton's body was thin to the extreme, her face drawn so tightly over her bone structure her sly smile was haunting. She'd been a strikingly pretty female and now exhibited a strange kind of beauty, ghostlike. *Vampire.*

Desi stepped back, quite involuntarily before her rational mind assured her vamps were but a myth. Shifters were real, as obviously were the Fae if most of the latter were now beyond this realm, but vampires were the stuff of childhood fairy tales. Scary tales. Michelle regarded her, an uneasy expression twisting her pretty face.

"Peyton was in the area and stopped by. She wants the Abbott in the window, but we don't have it in her size."

"Hello, Peyton." Desi ensured her tone was professional, natural. "Let me see what I can do."

"Desiree," the other woman purred. "Michelle tells me congratulations are in order."

"Thanks." No sense in prevaricating. No percentage in saying the best female won... Because she wasn't sure that was true and never would be.

A flash of teeth dazzled her for a moment before Peyton said, "I wanted to add him to my collection. Permanently. But it wasn't meant to be."

Suddenly desperate to know what transpired at Dawnfall, she fought her curiosity. "Apparently not. Are you around for the next week? Or should we send the dress to you?"

Peyton's eyes glowed, her wolf close to the surface, and Desi's own animal pressed hard in response. She'd never seen eyes that color before, a bluish red, and it took an effort not to flinch. But she'd never backed down in her life, so she maintained her smile and demeanor. Females didn't shift, with rare exceptions, and this wasn't one of them, despite the intense emotions making the very air thick and heavy.

"I'll be around," Peyton finally said. "I want to catch up with some shifters I met here before."

Did that include Tahl? Did she expect an invitation to dinner? The bitch wasn't setting foot in her house. Tahl's house. Unless she already had... "Enjoy your time in Blue Star. Leave your contact information with Michelle, would you? Nice seeing you again."

Her nose didn't grow and she wasn't cut down by lightning, so the blatant lie passed, even if Peyton visibly scoffed.

"I'll do that, Desiree. You take care." There was an implicit threat in that comment, evil licking along its edges.

"And you." Holding her composure, Desi moved back to her office, careful not to give any impression of retreat, at least outwardly. Peyton laughed, a high, brittle, tinkle of sound before Michelle spoke, asking for the information.

Carefully shutting the door, Desi considered her plan of action. Should she tell her mate Peyton Leaf was in town? There was no need, she decided. He'd hear about it soon enough and it hadn't really mattered to her. *Peyton? Yes, she stopped by the boutique, Tahl. I totally forgot.*

What had he said? That she didn't have to carry her burdens by herself anymore? Except this wasn't a burden. That shifter meant nothing in the scheme of things. Desi shivered. The other woman looked as though she ate small children for breakfast, nastiness oozing from every pore. Tahl would be vastly unhappy with her if he found out Desi had jinxed him, but Peyton would— She laughed out loud. Being fanciful again. Yet her skin still crawled and her wolf paced, alert and highly protective.

Jett should know that a member of another pack was in town. It was a courtesy for one to advise the Alpha, and surely River would have told her if she'd known Peyton was visiting. So she should tell her mate, as Jett's lieutenant he also should be made aware. Her mental gymnastics complete, she placed the call.

"Desi?" Pleasantly surprised described his response. She supposed she'd never called before.

"Hey. You probably don't know this, because if Jett knew he'd tell River and River would tell me—"

"Baby. Slow down."

Taking a deep breath, she said, "Peyton Leaf is here. Visiting."

Silence. The blood rushing through her veins

sang in her temples, and she realized she was holding her breath.

"*Stay away from her.* Close yourself in your office. I'll be right there."

Holy shit. He wasn't the boss of her, but damned if she didn't want to obey him. This once. Her rational mind protested the paternalism, but her animal embraced her role in the pack. "Okay."

"Desi, I can't tell you what it means that you're willing to listen to me."

It occurred that seeing them together might give her the answers she sought. "Don't get used to it," she muttered.

A short bark of a laugh echoed in her ear, followed by the slamming of a door. "I'll be there soon. I'll give you a call when I'm outside. Call me if she gets … difficult. Otherwise, stay off the line."

She analyzed his tone, alternately staring at the door and at her phone. He was rushing to see Peyton, but she'd detected no sense of excitement—maybe a little concern. *Call me if she gets difficult.* Something else, then, deeper than concern. Worry? Fear? *Dread,* her wolf offered up. That felt right, and way past a failed courtship, wasn't it? No matter why it failed…

It was awfully quiet in the main part of the store, and, slipping off her shoes, she moved silently to crack the door and peer through. Nothing moved in her narrow line of vision, so she pulled it wider. Michelle was unfolding some cashmere sweaters, holding one out for Peyton's perusal.

A scarlet tipped hand pinched the fabric between two fingers and Desi could feel the distaste all the way across the room.

"Maybe one of the vests?"

"Do I look like I hike? Maybe Desiree can tell us

when new merchandise is coming in."

About to venture out, her cell vibrated and she leaned sideways to the wall, out of eyeshot. "Hello?"

"I'm outside."

This had gone past a male trying to keep an ex and a current apart. "She's giving Michelle a hard time. I can't let it continue."

"Stay in the office. Please. At least for a few minutes."

"Okay." She didn't like it, but he'd said please.

Carefully easing the door nearly shut, she listened as she heard him enter.

"Tahl!" Michelle poured it on. "Desi's in the office."

"Hello, Peyton."

"Hello, Tahl!" Two words and they seethed with lust and something else she couldn't identify.

"That's right! You too know one another." Had Michelle actually clapped her hands?

It was like hearing a play unfold. Like merely a few days ago, Michelle hadn't rubbed Desi's nose in the fact he and Peyton had been an item. Tahl couldn't expect her to hide in the office. She hustled to get her shoes, stepping into them and making her way quietly into the store.

Michelle faded into the background as she focused on her mate and Peyton. Tahl's features were hard, his eyes narrowed, and strain was evident in his tense stance. The redhead, in contrast, was all sexy flutters.

"I'm surprised to see you here, Peyton."

Tossing all that hair, a near flame in the warmly lit display area, Peyton smiled, seduction visibly dripping. "I love to shop."

"But not in Blue Star. Not in pack territory that

isn't yours."

Pouting, the female laid a caressing hand on Tahl's arm. "That's old news. Years old."

"Etched in stone, Peyton. Does your grandfather know you're flouting pack law?"

"He's old too. His Council should be looking at a change. Looking to become a more progressive pack, like yours."

"And was his Council receptive to your ideas?" The implicit silky threat baffled Desi, but clearly not Peyton, who snatched her hand back.

"It's a work in progress."

"I'm sure it is. Now best you start the drive back. It gets dark early this time of year."

"I'll do that." Peyton stepped close to Tahl, going up on her toes in an effort to kiss him. He eased away and she stumbled to compensate. He didn't react to the look of fury that twisted her lovely face, but it made Desi shudder.

The other female stalked from the boutique, the door jangling and clattering behind her as if she sucked out all the air with her departure. Michelle whistled, an entirely unexpected reaction from someone so fussy.

Tahl's body relaxed a little, but Desi detected a certain agitation in her mate. He turned to follow Peyton, and she couldn't control her protest. It emerged as a faint, choking sound, but he heard.

"Hey." His gaze snapped to her and regret flashed over his features. Her heart sank. He really hadn't wanted her to witness that little meeting. And now he was going after the other female to have an additional conversation in private.

Instead, he said, "Almost closing time, Michelle. Head out, okay?"

Her stare bouncing between them, the other

woman nodded. "Sure. See you tomorrow."

Knowing the little incident would be all over the pack grapevine within minutes, Desi resigned herself. No point in making it worse. She forced a wide, happy smile and waved Michelle out. "Tomorrow. Don't be late!"

Into the quiet after her departure, Tahl said, "Sorry about that." Was that relief or disappointment in his voice? Desi couldn't tell. But he was here, with her, and the other female was long gone.

She lifted a shoulder. "I never had much use for Peyton anyhow. Not someone I want to spend time with."

"She shouldn't be in Blue Star."

"How come?"

"It was in our agreement." His eyes shuttered and she felt him close down.

"Agreement?"

Leaning against a rack, he rubbed his hand over his chin. Fine stubble rasped and her senses pricked. She waited, though wanted to press him before he could choose his words too carefully.

"In exchange for my help, Peyton wasn't to return here."

"What happened, Tahl?" She was afraid of the answer, but she had to know.

"What I felt … thought … well, it wasn't true." He looked her straight in the eye and she fell into the honesty brimming in that verdant green. "I realized the female I wanted wasn't Peyton."

Her belly flipped and cramped. *I hope you get what you need, regardless.* Maybe a person could interpret that curse differently. If what he thought about Peyton wasn't true, then she wasn't what he needed. But was *she*? Or had she changed Peyton somehow? Some weapon she'd turn out to be when she couldn't determine cause and effect. Her head ached, joining the party.

"Desi?"

"I can't say that I really understand. Okay, so she wasn't supposed to darken Blue Star's territory. Just her or all of those pack members?"

"I've said all I can say."

"Why'd you get so agitated about us coming face-to-face?"

He flat-out lied, and she read him clearly. "I guess I had visions of an incident, and wanted to head it off. Pack relations and all."

"Right." She imbued her answer with as much sarcasm as it could hold without crumbling under its own weight.

"Want to go out to dinner? Maybe stop by Jett and River's?"

Like a happily mated couple, doing stuff together around the elephant in the room—in their lives. Seeing as she was likely responsible for the behemoth, she shook her head. "I'll be home around six." She supposed it was her home. "I have a few things to finish up here."

"You're upset."

She sighed. "Tahl, our union isn't what one might call auspicious, what with the way it began. But I'm trying. I just need some space, is all."

He flinched. "I love you, baby. Know that if you know anything."

"You think you love me, Tahl," she said quietly. "Yet you followed Peyton."

"I was wrong, I told you. Sometimes we don't see what's in front of our noses."

"Or maybe something happens to change our minds. Something … unnatural."

"What do you know?" He stepped into her, looming, his wolf near the surface, and her heart skipped a beat, not that she was afraid of him. She cursed herself for skirting the truth so closely, for giving such a specific hint. Did he suspect? Was that why his wolf rose?

She backpedaled. "Nothing for sure, Tahl. It would be easier if I did." Tears welled and she blinked furiously.

"Ah, baby." He softened immediately. "Don't. It'll be fine. I know it."

Desi knew no such thing, but nodded and sniffed, turning to pull a tissue from the box on the counter while Tahl stroked her back. "I'm okay."

"Come with me to River and Jett's," he coaxed. "I need to talk to our Alpha and you haven't seen River in days. Leave your car in the lot. We can get it on the way back or I'll bring you in the morning."

"My mother might be home soon," she muttered. "And I won't need to come in."

"I can still drive you."

Conceding, she grabbed her things and followed him out, his tall, broad-shouldered form a calming beacon to her unsettled mind. She ensured her car was locked before climbing into his, noting that he waited, glancing around the lot.

Tipping her head back, she closed her eyes and worked on relaxing her tense muscles. By focusing on that, her mind quit chipping away and chasing its own tail.

Jett let them in, his blue gaze connecting with Tahl's emerald one, and they communicated in that mysterious way they had. Her brother looked at her next. "You okay, Desi?"

"I'm fine, Jett. Sometimes the past comes back to bite us in the ass."

He stared hard, looking behind her words, and then nodded. "River's upstairs with the kids."

Taking her cue, she hurried up the steps, hearing the men move toward Jett's study.

"… called Ashton …"

"… fucked up, Jett. She's…"

Out of earshot as they closeted themselves, she found her friend curled up on a wide, low bed, reading to Bella and Andrew.

"*Red Riding Hood*? Really, River."

"We're making our way through all the Grimm fairy tales."

"Red's a Grimm fairy tale?"

"If it isn't, it should be." River resumed reading when Andrew tugged at the book. He sounded out several of the words, and Desi didn't think it was from memory.

"He's reading already. Like Jett did."

"I know. He's figured out simple sums too, and understands things I didn't even think about until middle school."

"Fae blood," she mouthed, behind Andrew's back.

Abandoning the book to her son, with her daughter raptly watching his finger move across the printed word, River drew her to the chairs in the corner. "Tell me what happened."

"I have Fae blood too."

"What? I mean, I know. I was wondering about Peyton—"

Ignoring the clear invitation to share about the redhead, Desi said, "I suppose I was smarter than some. My grades were always good and I breezed through school."

"Okay." River peered at her. "What's this about?"

"My mother's legacy manifested differently in Jett, is all."

"Desi, tell me what you mean."

"Nothing, really. It's just that sometimes things come true when I want them to. Not bad things," she added hurriedly. "Not really. But I can't believe in coincidences forever."

River popped up and went to the intercom. She paged the nanny, and the young woman presented herself within moments. "Glenda, Desi and I need a few minutes alone."

"Sure, River. I'll watch them. No problem. If you want to move the laundry over in a bit?"

"Deal."

Desi loved the easy way River interacted with other shifters, at least most of them. There were a few, females mostly, who hadn't quite accepted their loss when Jett chose her. Glenda clearly didn't feel like she was an employee, but part of the household. Yet she showed River the deference due the Alpha's mate.

"Cassie's coming for a spell, so Glenda can take some time off." Her friend laughed quietly. "Andrew wears her out, though she loves him to pieces."

"You miss your sister."

"I do, and I wish she'd move here, but she wants to be there for Dad. So I'll take the time she'll give me! Let's head downstairs while the getting's good."

Once they were comfortable, sipping tea out in the yard, River fixed her with a look. "Spill."

"I'm pretty average."

With a snort, her friend said, "Right. Average. Nearly six feet tall, great body, beautiful, smart, successful, the Alpha's sister. Average."

"I mean average compared to Jett."

"Except?"

"Marlene doesn't want me to put it out there, and I haven't because I understand the implications. I'm not always sure it's even true. And she isn't either…"

"Desi, c'mon. What's happening?"

"I have an ability, at least that's what my mother calls it when the coincidences mount up. I guess I told her too many times about things that happened after I said something to people who upset me."

"I don't get it."

"Me neither. I just know to watch what I say, even joking."

"Not helping."

Ticking situations off, Desi shared six specific events that came to mind where her response seemed to impact the recipient. "There might be more." She didn't share her concern about Tahl and Peyton.

"Marlene thinks you have some kind of power?" There was no skepticism in the other woman's tone. She'd met Marlene, after all. Not human. Not shifter.

"She does. And sometimes, so do I. It weighs on me." She set her cup down and got up to pace to the fence separating the yard from the woods. Jett had cleared a swath and outfitted it with security devices since the rogue alpha had breached the perimeter.

River's little hand touched her arm. "I can imagine. Except you're not a vindictive person."

Turning to face her friend, she said, "I hope I'm not."

"When did it manifest?"

"I'm not sure. Maybe late high school? It might have been earlier except in the chaos of adolescence I probably didn't notice that I turned somebody's life upside down."

"It doesn't sound like that's what happened."

A bitter laugh choked her throat. "They got what was coming to them, you mean?"

"In a fair world, yes. People don't always get

caught when they do bad stuff, so it's kind of nice for me to hear that they get theirs."

That was a new perspective, except she didn't fancy herself as some kind of one-woman vigilante. "I don't want it, but I'm stuck with it."

"Does Tahl know?"

"No!" She bit her lip, but the vehemence had been involuntary.

River stepped back, worry creasing her brow and darkening her eyes. "He wouldn't think less of you, or judge you, Desi."

All in, she said, "Even if I changed the outcome of his relationship with Peyton Leaf?"

As a conversation stopper, it was a doozy, because River blinked, opened her mouth, then shut it. Twice.

"Exactly."

"Wait. What could you possibly have said—I mean you *say* it, right?" At Desi's nod, she continued, "What could you have said to change the outcome? You didn't even know he was interested in her. Not that he was, for real, apparently…"

"You see? It's so freaking convoluted. It makes my head hurt. He went there, he stayed there and then he came back and settled for me."

"Oh, Desi. It has to hurt, regardless. And being so uncertain…"

"It blisters, River. Scalds. Kicks my self-worth in the face. But the guilt is worse."

"I got sidetracked," the other woman insisted. "What did you say to him?"

"*Regardless, I hope you get what you need.* It's etched in my brain like it was yesterday. I might have congratulated him too." She shook, disclosing her deepest, most shameful secret, but there was a certain relief—and dark satisfaction—in sharing.

Head shaking from side to side, River pursed her lips. "I think he needed you."

"I was bitter. And vindictive. That's not how I meant it."

"What did you mean?"

"Back then? I sure didn't mean for him to get his needs met, not past the physical. I figured if he couldn't see past the trappings to the nasty center, he deserved her. She was pure trouble during the time she and Alpha Leaf were here. Caused fights between the young males, intimidated and bullied the females and generally stirred things up, although getting others to deal with it at the time fell short. It was almost like it didn't even mean anything until afterward when friendships had to be rebuilt and amends made. It's a testimony to Jett's rule that she didn't have the effect she might have had."

"You were pretty young, Desi."

"I was devastated."

"I'm still not feeling it."

"Well, it doesn't matter, because I'm not telling him. He chose me, second string or not, and we're stuck. I'm making the best of it, though being second choice stings. I don't know what I hoped to accomplish, telling you. Sorry."

"Friends confide in one another," River chided. "You know my secret."

She hugged the other woman, wrapping her up. "Thanks, hun. I love you too. And I do feel a bit lighter."

As they moved back to their tea, River said, "My guess Marlene didn't want anyone to know your potential. So it wouldn't get misused."

"That's it, exactly. And we're not sure, exactly how it works, so it's best left quiet."

"Jett should know."

"Not something you can keep from him?"

"He won't use you, Desi. He's not like that."

"He'll be pissed, but we'll figure it out." She sagged into a chair. "Tahl's going to find out."

"I think you want him to know."

"Not."

"He's not likely to think you … influenced him."

"Well, he'll be on the lookout now, won't he? It'll make things more awkward than they are now. I shouldn't have told you."

"I won't tell Jett until Marlene gets home. You can have a family meeting—and you might want to find a way to tell Tahl beforehand."

"He's family now too, isn't he? Maybe he did get one thing he needed, anyhow."

"Self-pity, Desi?"

"I waffle between self-pity and loathing."

"You have a caring mate, a stable pack, and a pup on the way."

"It'll have to be enough," she agreed. *This whole situation should feel divorced from reality…*

"We'll talk again, but I see Jett looking out the kitchen window, and he'll be eavesdropping. Let's put together some dinner and we can at least share some relaxed time."

Chapter Ten

Tahl couldn't shake the deep sense of foreboding that tainted the time spent with his Alpha and his family. The kids made everyone laugh, the meal a noisy, happy time. Desiree lightened up and even treated her brother with something like her usual style. Maybe she was going to forgive Jett after all, and he dared hope she might come to forgive him. He'd been living on hope for what felt like forever, and it wasn't a particularly fulfilling meal, as fickle as it seemed.

His mate occasionally gave him quick, sideways glances and he sensed her speculation. Jett had cautioned him about saying anything further, at least until he could talk with Alpha Leaf, who wasn't taking his calls. So his foreboding likely had a solid base. Peyton was on the edge, he could feel it, and he should have done something about that and to hell with the agreement.

"Unca Tahl?" Andrew had slipped from his chair to crawl beneath the table and pop up between Tahl's knees. The toddler stared up at him, the assessing look in his pale blue eyes at odds with the childlike features. Tahl blinked.

"What's up, little guy?" He tapped the child gently on the bicep.

"What's wrong?"

One didn't talk down to this child, though Andrew could lose himself in play with enthusiasm, being every bit a kid. "Thinking heavy thoughts, Andrew."

"Like sacks of sand?" Jett had just filled a sandbox for the kids, and Tahl well remembered the heft of those bags.

"About as heavy."

"You should tell Desi." Andrew nodded as if announcing something vastly important.

Making himself smile, he nodded back. "I should."

"She's your mate, now. Like my mom and my dad." The slightest childish lisp didn't detract from the solemn observation.

"She is, buddy." He leaned forward, and whispered, "I love her lots."

One chubby hand touched his face, right beneath his temple. "Me too."

When he looked up, the adults were staring, even Desiree, although her gaze wasn't full of warmth and understanding. No, she looked sad—and suddenly weary.

"Time to head out, Desi?"

River instantly demurred. "There's dessert. Something chocolate."

Bella and Andrew cheered, and he forced another smile. "Can't pass that up."

After dessert, and over coffee, Jett's cell sounded an alert and he grabbed for it, ignoring River's reproachful look. "It's important, sweetheart."

Motioning to Tahl, he led the way to the study, shutting the door against anyone else. "It's Ashton," he said and put it on speaker.

The old shifter's voice crackled in the space. "We called an emergency session, Jett. I didn't know she was there. Mind you, I thought we had her under control before she left, too, so I suppose I should have known she'd head over to Blue Star."

"Has she returned?" Tahl knew he should have followed her, should have had called another shifter to ensure she returned to Dawnfall. He was the only one here who was immune to Peyton when she wasn't medicated, however, so sending another pack member would have been irrelevant—or a disaster. It didn't detract from the fact he hadn't been able to leave Desiree.

"Not yet. It's a fair distance, so maybe she'll be here soon."

Or she had no intention of returning… He cleared his throat. "It's Tahl Powers, Alpha."

"Hello, Tahl. I sorry for this. I know we agreed—"

"Is she back to the way she was?" He couldn't even say it out loud. His throat and shoulder ached as if in sympathy.

"I'm not sure," the old man admitted. "Peyton's adept at hiding herself from others, and the medication is very helpful in that regard. I'm wondering if she was even using it, though the people I have taking care of her believe that's not the case."

"Could she be getting resistant?" Jett interjected.

"Possible. Though our doctor monitors her regularly. She got up this morning, like usual, dressed and had breakfast, same old routine. Went out for a walk and ditched her bodyguard. Simply vanished and somehow found transportation."

Tahl's gut closed in on itself, a thoroughly nasty sensation that he could hardly speak around. "Do you think—"

With a harsh bark of laughter, Alpha Leaf said, "I can't see it being anything else, can you? You should have dealt with her when you saw her today."

Peyton was this man's granddaughter, his only living relative, seeing as his mate had passed not long before and Peyton's mother had perished in a suspicious house fire. It made what appeared to be a callous comment highly significant. But Tahl remembered what it had been like to live in that situation for nearly two years, and he hadn't had the same exposure as the older shifter…

"I couldn't," was all he said. *I had to put my mate before duty.*

"Not your responsibility," Ashton conceded. "If Peyton isn't here within the hour, I'm heading your way, if you have no objection, Jett."

"Who will you bring?"

"My guards, not that they'll be much use."

They finalized the arrival times and established that Aston and his shifters would use The Sanctuary, the safe house now standing empty.

"You and Desi should stay here."

His wolf threw down, all of his senses on alert, and he cursed. "We shouldn't have come here at all. Goddamn it, Jett. Your mate and your kids are here."

"Then it's good you are too."

His Alpha's practicality grounded him, and the relief made him nauseous. Swallowing, he said thoughtfully, "She was pissed, but not out of control, Jett. Not like I remember. And Michelle wasn't influenced. Nor Desiree. It could be Ashton is overreacting a little."

"Except she flouted the rules and came here. After you. And I doubt she brought any of her meds with her. That's obsession."

There was that. And who knew how Peyton's troubled mind worked? "She might have returned to Dawnfall."

"Well, best we prepare if not."

"I'm still not certain being here is the best plan. I should leave Desi with you and head home. Her car is at the shop and Peyton might check that out, not find anything, and go to my house." He was back to thinking he'd made a big mistake coming here. He could have dropped his mate off and conversed with Jett over the phone. He'd just wanted to give Desi what she needed.

"Tahl. Find my lieutenant." Jett's voice cut like a whip through his frenzied thinking.

With a deep breath, he replied, "I'm back, Alpha." He now fully understood how a threat to River—a very real threat—had nearly stripped Jett of his focused ability to rule his pack in the short term.

"Good. Now, what are you thinking?"

"I'm leaving my mate here. Peyton has no idea where you live." He didn't think, although the meetings had been held here. "But she's been at my place. I'm heading there as soon as I talk to Desiree."

"You think splitting up is a good idea?"

Did he? He was desperate to keep Desi safe, but instinct told him Peyton would go where she believed he'd be. His mate might be in her sights, but it stood to reason that where he was, so would Desi be. And if he was concerned for nothing, all the better. "If she can't get in, she's no risk."

Jett nodded, accepting his assessment and Tahl refused to second-guess himself. With a curt nod, he went to find his mate.

She was near the couch, Bella and Andrew on either side of her, singing something about Tony Chestnut knowing they loved you, complete with actions. He studied the picture she made, envisioning her with their pups, and found it hard to speak past the lump in his throat.

"What's going on?" River asked from her perch by the window. Desi stopped singing, mid-chorus, but the kids' pure, childish tones continued. *Toe knee nose.*

Motioning Desi over, he said quietly to both females, "I'm heading out for a bit. Business."

Two pairs of eyes bored into him, but he maintained a calm demeanor and must have conveyed it well because they both relaxed.

"Can you drop me off?" Desi looked around, presumably for her purse.

"No."

She blinked, and he hurried to qualify. "I'll come back. If that's okay."

"I knew I should have brought my car."

River stepped up. "You know you're welcome here, Desi. I want some adult time after the kids go down."

"Sure." His mate gave him another searching look before nodding.

He grasped her arm and tugged her close. He loved her height, not having to bend and dip to kiss her. Except Desi didn't allow him to kiss her. Regardless, he leaned in and managed to brush his mouth over hers. For a fraction of a second, her lips softened before she disengaged.

"I'll see you later."

When he reached the doorway, he glanced back to see her watching him. Sad was becoming her usual expression when her guard wasn't up, and regret tinged his belief that they were meant to be together.

Taking care to examine his surroundings, he let himself out of the house, hearing River lock up behind him, knowing his Alpha would be double-checking. Climbing into the Camaro, he drove to his house, vigilant for lights that might be in proximity. Seeing nothing, he turned onto his street.

An unfamiliar vehicle was parked up against the curb, unoccupied, unless the occupant or occupants had ducked out of sight. He pulled in the drive and studied the house. A small figure huddled on the wicker love seat and flame-red hair glowed with subtlety beneath the porch light.

She'd been there long enough for the motion sensors to have shut off, but that didn't give him a timeline. He counted himself lucky that she hadn't tried to search him out, again indulging in a recrimination that earlier he'd simply let her go.

"Peyton. I thought you were heading home." He watched her carefully, noting the frenetic flush and claw-like hands. His heart sank.

"I was. And then I thought I had to see you again. I felt … compelled." She uncoiled her slender length to drift in his direction and he braced himself.

Her signature fragrance reached him, a mixture of roses and lavender. It conjured up a plethora of bad memories and he shook them off, raising his palm. She halted, full lips thinning as she visibly tried to control her rage. Her blue eyes glowed violet and despite his best effort, he was drawn to her.

"Invite me in, Tahl. We should talk." She glanced behind him. "I see your … mate isn't here."

The mention of Desiree renewed his strength and determination, and the other female's hold on him weakened and melted away. He needed to keep Peyton under wraps until her grandfather arrived, but how? He didn't want her in his home again. "I don't think so. We could get a coffee."

"I thought you preferred to keep shifter business away from humans."

The threat wove through her words, and he shrugged, knowing she wouldn't be above creating a scene, perhaps one that couldn't be explained away. Or something worse. He opened the door, feeling her right at his shoulder, far too close, and ushered her inside.

Heading to the kitchen, he took out his cell. "Have a seat. Can I make coffee?"

"I'll take wine."

Of course, she would. He texted Jett while pretending to search for a bottle. Pouring her a glass, he decided on a beer, not that he'd drink it, and took the beverages to the living room.

Peyton was wandering about, stopping to consider the items Desi had set out, her upper lip twitching in a near snarl. She threw him a glance before sauntering to take a seat. She patted the couch as he set her wine in front of her.

He took the chair closest to the door and waited. Thwarted, she narrowed her eyes before reaching for the glass. She made a production out of the first sip, and objectively he could understand how she drew men so effortlessly. Even without the compulsion she spun.

"You mated the Alpha's sister. How forward thinking of you, Tahl." Her innocent look belied the malice of her comment.

He smiled and took a mouthful of beer. "How's your grandfather?"

Lifting a thin shoulder, she then tucked a sheaf of hair behind one ear. The gesture, like everything Peyton did, was studied, calling attention to her glossy auburn mane and her perfect profile. "Like I said, he's getting old. Stuck in his ways."

Knowing the kind of progressiveness she favored, he contented himself with a nod. Peyton wanted to introduce something quite radical—to rule and conquer.

"I expect you called him?"

"He's hoping you're on your way home." A partial truth, it appeared to satisfy her.

"Come back with me, Tahl." She leaned forward, palms outstretched imploringly, cleavage on display.

"You know I can't do that, Peyton."

"Because you chose to mate," she spat, her fingers curling into claws.

The very air crackled with tension and the hair on his arms lifted. Peyton smirked, her pale skin nearly translucent against her red lips. "There's no guarantee of a long and happy life, is there, Tahl? Not for anyone."

"Don't threaten what's mine," he gritted, as she unerringly put her finger on his worst fear.

"I never threaten, Tahl." She stood, waving a languid arm, even as her gaze shot to the door. "You need to come back. With me. To me."

Shaking his head, he heard voices outside but received no warning as Peyton launched herself at him.

****

Jett checked his phone, obviously reading a text, and Desi read his body language. River was upstairs with Bella and Andrew. "What's wrong?"

"Nothing. Tahl just checked in."

"And?"

"And he'll be delayed a while."

"I should go. It's been a long day." She couldn't stop thinking about Peyton now she wasn't distracted.

"Hang around for a bit," he advised. No, he ordered her again. There was no mistaking it.

"He's gone to meet her," she stated.

"Desi."

She looked him in the eye. "I'm not worried about him fucking her, Jett. Not unless something's changed with shifter nature." *Unless I changed it ... paranoia will destroy yuh.*

"You okay?" Her brother stepped closer. "You looked ... funny."

"A stupid thought," she said, dismissing his concern. He'd know soon enough once he and River talked.

Her sister-in-law wandered into the great room as if summoned. "The urchins are asleep and Glenda's upstairs reading. I thought we might talk."

She'd done enough talking today. More than enough. "I'm tired, River. Sorry."

Jett stared, and opened his mouth when his cell rang. Saved by the bell.

"She's here," he said, after greeting a male voice she couldn't identify. He turned, moving fast, but she heard him say. "At Tahl's."

She grabbed her purse and was hot on his heels, ignoring River's wide eyes.

Her brother shook his head as he ended the call. "Stay here."

"No. And don't pull either the big brother card or the Alpha one on me either, Jett."

He loomed, despite her height, but she faced him down.

"Take her with you, Jett." River wrung her hands but looked resolute. "I don't know what this is about, but Desi can take care of herself. Trust me."

"River," she warned. She had no control. What should she do? Tell Peyton to drop dead or something?

He studied them both, his gaze settling on his mate, and Desi knew he was reading her mind. He muttered under his breath. *Females.* They both ignored him. "Can you follow orders if you come? Like if I tell you to stay in the vehicle, you stay?"

"I can." She wouldn't promise to follow them, though was capable of doing so. Witness how she'd obeyed Tahl today. Mostly.

"River, lock up. Benjamin will be here shortly to keep an eye. Stay inside."

"I promise. You'll be okay?"

He yanked her against him, big arms enveloping her much smaller body, and Desi had to look away at the caring and passion that flared between them they kissed.

"I'll be fine." River's voice was a tad shaky.

They took his big SUV, and she scrambled into the passenger seat to keep up, as he powered down the drive. As they drove, she asked, "Jett, can you tell me what's going on?"

Keeping his gaze on the road, he said, "If it all goes well, there will be no reason for you to know, Desiree. You'll have to trust me on this."

Maybe she'd have to set her curiosity aside, especially when Jett spoke in his Alpha voice. She knew better than to mess around with him. "Okay."

"Do you want to enlighten *me*?"

"No." She didn't need to ask what he was referring to. She wished she hadn't said anything to River. The time would come soon enough when she'd have to come clean, but Marlene would be home and she could be part of that conversation. It gave her some comfort.

They drew up to Tahl's just as a pickup truck arrived. Jett jumped out and went over to greet an older male who disembarked from the passenger side. A much larger shifter clambered from the extended back and was joined by another, nearly identical male, and the two flanked the first.

Alpha Leaf. Desi recognized him. Jett hadn't told her to stay in the SUV, so she slipped down out and went to stand behind her brother. The other Alpha glanced at her and spared a nod before focusing on Jett.

"She was waiting for him when Tahl got home. I expect he's keeping her entertained until you could get here."

Desi wondered at his choice of words, but said nothing, picking up on the tension.

"Best I head straight in, then. She's a trial even when she's not off her meds," Alpha Leaf grunted.

Meds? Maybe that explained Peyton's overall agitation. She had some kind of mental health issue. Desi stayed quiet, as the older male headed toward the front door. His bodyguards closed ranks behind him and Jett followed, albeit at a distance. It seemed a lot of big males to take one small female home.

She watched as Alpha Leaf froze at the door then pushed inside without knocking on the distinct sound of a scuffle. The guards jostled to gain entrance, and she saw one go down, then the other. Jett cursed and hurdled their prone bodies, only to falter and sink to his knees.

What the fuck? Desi pushed forward, scrambling over the big men, pushing Jett to one side as she saw Alpha Leaf grappling with Peyton, who was somehow gaining the upper hand.

Long hair flowing like a flame, the other female hissed and lashed out at her grandparent. Were those claws? And teeth? The redhead slashed the old shifter's neck, blood spurting in a gruesome arc and Desi bit back a scream. Where was Tahl?

She staggered forward, her animal warring between fight and flight, and spied him lying beyond the combatants, on the floor. He lay still and slack, and terror gripped to infuse her entire being with adrenaline. Lunging, she made it to him in two long strides and knelt to run her hands over him, cradling his head in her palms.

Blood soaked his shirt, muting the faint rise and fall of his chest, and she felt his erratic pulse. Worried he'd bleed out, unconscious and unable to shift, she ripped the material open, buttons popping in a weird pinging counterpoint to the growls and snarls behind her. Deep gashes met her stare and she packed them with the cloth, searching for the injury that had laid her mate out.

A dark bruise fanned out from his temple and over his forehead and she saw the marble figurine she'd placed on an end table only a few nights ago, lying nearby, the base bloody. Tahl didn't respond, even when she tapped his cheek and pinched his ear. His breathing became fainter. "Wake up," she hissed. "Please, Tahl."

She couldn't lose him. It didn't matter if he hated her for what she'd done, for how she'd treated him. She promised to be the best mate ever if he would just wake up and not die. Staring at her bloody hands, she swallowed a scream. Her vision had come true, another curse. She pressed her mouth against his and whimpered. Cold.

The old shifter crashed to the floor, and Peyton screamed victoriously. Desi forced herself to face the other woman, trying not to quail. Face streaked with blood and gore, canines glinting ominously, Peyton smiled horribly as she casually brushed a bloody tendril of hair from her cheek.

Her speech impacted by those teeth, she lisped, "He wants you? He can have you, but certainly not alive."

"You killed him." Desi hardly recognized her own voice, wooden with despair.

"He's not dead, bitch. Not yet. If he concedes and becomes my consort, I'll let him live. But he can't join me with you in the picture."

Slowly gaining her feet, she stared at Peyton. "Consort?"

The scent of blood was cloying and Desi swayed, even as the other female confirmed it. "They tried to keep me a secret. Like I was something shameful. I'm vampire, Desiree. Well, half. The better half. Better than wolf shifters."

"What have you done to Jett?" She could have bitten her tongue out, drawing attention to him like that, but she needed information.

With a graceful shrug, despite her blood-soaked appearance, Peyton said, "I compelled him. And them, my grandfather's guards. I haven't wasted my time locked up, taking the medications for my so-called psychosis. All to keep the secret."

She had nothing in common with this, this, shifter hybrid, Desi decided, regardless they both kept secrets. Mind-numbing fear filled her over her baby. She couldn't let this crazy bitch win. Her child was going to live.

"I'm not going to let you hurt anyone else." *Or take Tahl.*

On another dreadful laugh, Peyton sneered. "I can't compel females as easily, or you'd be dead already. But no one is going to stop me. I'm going to rule. Maybe starting here, instead of Dawnfall. With Tahl, if he chooses me over death."

"No." That darkness descended again, this time imbuing her with a strange sense of confidence and well-being, as though she was in control. Peyton came at her, wild and insane, and Desi's vision narrowed to that one sole focus.

She flowed, seamlessly, to meet the other female, taking her down in a flurry of limbs. She heard herself growl at the sting of claws, the prick of teeth, but those things felt distant and trifling. Using her superior strength and weight, she persevered. There was a resounding crack and Peyton flailed once with a soundless scream Desi heard in the deep recesses of her being, and then lay boneless beneath her.

"Holy fuck." Jett urged her aside, throwing his shirt over Peyton's face, those wide eyes staring.

Tahl groaned and the room brightened around her, colors becoming evident. Desi crawled to him as he pushed up, his eyes widening as he took her in. "Baby," he rasped.

She shook as he awkwardly embraced her, aware her clothes were but mere rags, hanging from her body.

"She fucking shifted," Jett murmured, his voice incredulous. "She shifted and took down Peyton."

His voice rumbling in his chest beneath her cheek, Tahl said, "Is Peyton…"

Alpha Leaf struggled to his knees, and Desi closed her eyes against the sight of his torn flesh. He was already healing, as Alphas were wont to do, far quicker than ordinary shifters, but he'd been badly injured.

The old male said, "She's not dead. Not unless your female took her head. That's one story that's not a myth. It's how I dispensed of her father, though it took half a dozen males to manage it in an ambush. Peyton's likely incapacitated. For now."

"She can't be allowed this opportunity again, Ashton," Jett spoke quietly, but his warning was clear.

"I know. I know. She's my flesh and blood, but a monster. Her father wanted to rule as well. It can't be allowed. Not another attempt at insurrection. We'll take care of it." He motioned to his guards who were now on their feet, groggy, but functioning.

"She can't compel you."

"Nor Tahl," Ashton replied. "We share DNA, so I expect that's why. As for your lieutenant, well, she made the mistake of trying to turn him and instead made him immune. We figured that out and he stayed in Dawnfall to help us get back on track. And manage Peyton. We owe him for keeping our secret. And you. But you must know all that."

"I do, although not the details."

Desi wanted to know the details or maybe she didn't. It was sinking in that she had *shifted*. In extremis, but she'd *shifted*. And that maybe she hadn't influenced Tahl and Peyton's relationship at all. Her brain worked busily, sifting and sorting, at odds with her wolf who was bewildered yet complacent.

Without an ounce of energy, she watched as the big shifters carefully secured Peyton's unconscious body, taking care to not only bind her limbs but blindfold and gag her. *Vampire.* Her body announced various aches and pains, small hurts and bigger ones. Tahl soothed her, sensing her discomfort.

He made no move to assist with Peyton, and Jett escorted the group outside, pausing only to cast them a glance and say, "I'll see you both tomorrow. You and Marlene. We need to decide if Council should meet."

Shutting the door behind him, his footsteps diminished and vehicles started up. Silence reigned.

"Let me see you."

"No." She hid her face against his chest and curled in tighter.

"C'mon, baby. We need to get up. Jett will send the doctor and better he knows what he has to treat."

"No." She might still be furry. She wished she could recall… Or maybe not.

Groaning, he pushed up to his knees, pulling her with him. "I'm fucked up. Damn her."

Unwilling to make him struggle, she clambered to her feet, helping him stand. He touched his forehead and winced. "There's two of you. That's the good news."

"And the bad?"

"My head might explode."

They staggered toward the bathroom, clutching one another before Tahl halted. "I have to set the alarm."

"Unless you think she's coming back, I think it's okay." She doubted locked and armed doors and windows would deter that hybrid in any event and hoped the deed had been done, as distasteful as it would have been. She felt a flicker of sympathy for the grandfather.

He locked the door and punched in the code before making his way back to her. Knowing she'd almost lost him made her sway and he grabbed her elbows. "Hang in there, baby. Where are you hurt?"

His own injuries were beginning to clot, the bleeding stopped, although the massive bruise on his face was very evident.

"I don't know."

Walking her into the bathroom, he stripped the remnants of her clothing away, inspecting her under the bright light. She cautiously opened her eyes and examined her reflection. Her hair was a mess, tangled and damp. Blood covered her skin in weird patterns, some areas protected by fabric, others not so much.

There was a gash near the base of her throat, mostly on a collar bone, and a few slices on her right bicep. Some tiny holes that could only have come from Peyton's canines dotted her cheek and other shoulder. None of her wounds bled very much. No sign of fur.

Tahl turned the shower on and stripped down himself, his eyes troubled and his features strained. He urged her into the tub and stepped in beside her, yanking the curtain shut. The warm water coursed through her hair and over her body, making her wince when it traversed the raw skin.

Pooling pink around her feet, she suppressed a shudder at the sight and closed her eyes to tilt her face into the spray. When she opened them again, Tahl was studying her. "What?"

"You shifted."

"I'm a freak."

"Baby. You shifted and saved us all." He laid a hand on her belly. "All of us."

Reaction hit and she shivered, despite the warmth. Tahl cursed and quickly lathered her up, taking care with the more obvious damage. She stood, feet splayed and head down as he cleansed her, not even protesting when he used her body wash on her hair.

Hurriedly doing the same, he then helped her out and clumsily wrapped her in a towel, working a smaller one over her head, before grabbing one for himself.

"Wait here while I snag your robe."

She sank onto the closed toilet seat and put Peyton's twisted features out of her mind, for now, studying her fingernails, thankfully free of blood. She'd shifted. Saying it over and over didn't make it any less impressive—and freaky.

"Leave the towels around you." He drew her to her feet and bundled her into her robe, tying it over the bulk of fabric. He'd stopped to pull on sleep pants, his impressive chest still bare, his wounds healing.

Desi reached out and traced the old scar at the base of his throat. "She did this."

"She did and infused it with her own blood so it would scar. Mark me as hers. Tried to turn me, but it didn't work."

She stared into his eyes. "Did she compel you when she was here the first time?"

"She did, although I think it was partly a form of hypnosis. She obviously honed her craft to take the guards and Jett down, and nearly deal with her grandfather."

"So you didn't—"

"I didn't follow her to Dawnfall because I'd fallen for her, Desi. I followed because I had to. I felt I had no choice, although it didn't feel horrible. Not until I saw who she really was."

"And you couldn't tell me when you came back?"

"I promised Alpha Leaf. She led a nearly successful take-over back then, and I foiled it. He had ground to recoup and fences to build. If his pack thought she was a real danger, they'd have killed her and he hoped to avoid that. He loves her. And if word spread about vampires infesting shifter packs, we'd be at war. There would be purges. Anyone different would be in the crosshairs. Like, Jett. And you. Marlene."

Tears swelled and spilled to wash over her cheeks and he groaned. "Don't fucking cry. Don't. I did what I had to do, Desi. And I came back for you. It'll work out."

She welcomed his embrace and let him simply hold her, knowing they had a great deal to talk about and that it would have to wait.

Chapter Eleven

She'd fallen asleep in Tahl's arms, in his big bed, still swathed in those towels and her robe, and she'd never felt closer to him. Her slumber had been surprisingly sound, without even a flicker of a nightmare, though the stuff of those surely lingered, waiting to pounce. She hadn't allowed herself to think about Peyton when she awoke, and Tahl hadn't made any effort to remind her. Her wounds had mostly healed, although Tahl still looked battered.

And now they were driving to her brother's. She nursed a go-cup of strong coffee, if decaffeinated, flavored the way she liked it, compliments of her mate. An awkward silence replaced the nearly comfortable one they'd mutually employed while getting ready for the meeting their Alpha demanded. Neither seemed to have to energy to broach the subject and in her case, she was now only too willing to wait.

Tahl hadn't treated her any differently, despite the fact he must have seen her in wolf form, or at least partly shifted, and while that lurked hugely at every turn, she found she couldn't raise it. She was a total coward, she decided, unable to face any of the things that made her different.

Marlene's car was already there, and Desi realized she hadn't even thought to contact her mother. Tahl had been all she needed. Her belly clenched when she considered how vulnerable that made her. Did he still love her? Could he?

Parking near the door, he turned the engine off and faced her. The mounting tension reflected deep in his emerald eyes, but he spoke quietly. "Ready?"

"As I'll ever be."

She unlatched her seatbelt and he was out and around the car to open her door. A young male shifter loitered nearby and Tahl sketched a wave. "That's Benjamin Kraft."

"He's all grown up." And what a handsome young male he was, indeed. She made herself smile at him, and he nodded back before scanning the area. He gave the impression of being lazily alert if there was such a thing. Like a younger Tahl.

"I trained him and think he's the best we have. He's been charged with watching out for the kids and River, or them and the nanny, whenever they leave the house."

He was probably waiting on them now, she decided. On cue, the front door opened and Andrew and Bella flew through it, a young female in hot pursuit. Not Glenda, but a pretty blonde.

River had said her sister was coming for a visit, and the girl must have arrived first thing this morning. The timing sucked, in a way, but at least she wouldn't be listening in, and she was wonderful with the kids.

Cassie Fortuna gathered Bella up and hip checked Andrew gently toward the SUV, even as Benjamin hustled to intercept the little boy. Desiree forgot her worries and ran over to hug both children, viscerally aware she might have lost her chance to ever see them again, after last night.

"Going with Aunt Cassie for pancakes and waffles," Andrew announced, beaming at her and letting her kiss his nose.

"Wawles." Bella crooned.

"Sweet girl, you have lots of whipped cream," she said, kissing a chubby cheek, soaking in the baby scent.

"Hi, Desi." Cassie gave her a shy smile and

flickered a look toward Tahl. "Congratulations."

"Thank you." Her quiet acceptance was heartfelt and Tahl gripped her hand.

She helped Andrew inside the SUV, buckling him in, and then reached for Bella. Cassie's cheeks were scarlet, her eyes wide, as Benjamin took the child from her arms to hand her over. Desi looked between the two young shifters and hid a smile.

Cassie was a few years from her mating heat, but that didn't mean she wasn't recognizing the potential of a fine male. A pang resonated in her chest when she recalled being exactly that age and head over heels for Tahl.

Casting a critical look over Benjamin, a few years older than Cassie, she hoped he didn't break her heart.

She stood with Tahl, watching as they drove away, wishing fervently she'd gone for waffles too if only to avoid the people still inside.

"We should go in," he said quietly.

Get it over and done with, she told herself. "I guess so."

The house was noticeably quiet when they gained entrance, Jett looking inscrutable while River studied them with a wary expression. Just as Desi's spirits crashed, her friend rushed over and slid her arms around her.

"Oh goddess, Desi. I don't have the words. Jett told me last night, but he wouldn't let me go over or even call you." She slanted an angry glance in her mate's direction.

"She had her mate, River." Her brother's quiet assertion silenced her friend, but she hugged harder.

Marlene sauntered in from the back of the house, a tall, thin man close behind. Desi blinked, forgetting to bask in the comforting hold of River who clearly wasn't repulsed or shocked by whatever Jett had described.

The male with her mother held himself regally, dark hair smoothly brushed, face cleanly shaved, his fit body covered in casual, but expensive clothes. He met her stare with one of his own, and she felt a spark of connection.

Tahl stepped close, his arm wrapping around her waist, and he studied the newcomer.

"This is Simon Hancock," Marlene said. "He's much older than I am and has learned to hide his Fae and manage his abilities. I met him last year on a buying trip—he's based in New York but prefers to avoid all that glass and steel, for obvious reasons."

Simon didn't look a day over fifty, near her mother's age, and Desi wondered how old he really was. He had Fae blood, of that there was no doubt, now she studied him. Not that humans would notice, and maybe not many shifters.

He nodded to her and Tahl but didn't offer his hand. "It is good to meet you." The syntax of his speech was off, somehow. Dated.

"Hello."

Tahl merely nodded, and she felt his watchfulness.

"After spending time with Simon, I decided to ask him to sit in as we discuss last night's events."

Tahl gave his Alpha a sharp glance but didn't dispute him, not that he would in front of anyone else, she surmised. If her mother and Jett were comfortable with Simon, then she was. She squeezed Tahl's hand in reassurance and he relaxed a little.

Gathered around the long table used for Council meetings, she squirmed beneath the stares. "Can we just put it out there? Peyton is—hopefully, *was*—some kind of vampire shifter who set her sights on Tahl, who obliged her only to find out who she really was so he backed off. He helped the Dawnfall Alpha put things back together, kept the vampire thing a secret, came home and uh, pursued me. We're mates now. Except Peyton didn't get the message and came looking for Tahl who she thought should be part of some grand plan to rule her grandfather's pack and any other pack she fancied. I didn't care for that idea, so I went furry and took her down. End of story."

River hid a smile, as did Marlene, but the men looked at her as though she was insane. "What? So there're a few gaps, but I can't fill those in." Well, except for one piece she deliberately left out.

"We're all pretty much on the same page about Peyton, Desiree. Tahl was compelled by her and sacrificed a couple years of his life to help repair the damage. But it's important you realize the implications impacting Blue Star."

"I know, Jett. I get it." She looked at her mother. "It would only have been a matter of time before you and me, and Jett—probably Lizbeth too—would have been regarded as a threat to the status quo if Peyton wasn't contained."

"Tradition," Marlene muttered. "You call yourself progressive, Jett, and yet you hide your Fae side."

"And for good reason, Marlene," Simon interjected. "Shifters accept their differences, celebrate them, from what I understand, but remain reserved from humans. We all know why. They wouldn't want that status disturbed."

To Desi's surprise, her mother didn't formulate any kind of argument, probably because there was really nothing to dispute.

Tahl had situated himself close to her, one big

hand resting on her thigh, a heavy, comforting weight. She decided to use that as a barometer when the next revelation was discussed.

"Do we know if Alpha Leaf took care of the situation?" River was trying to be delicate, and Desi searched for a softer feeling regarding the redheaded hybrid but couldn't locate one. The female had planned to kill her and her brother, her unborn child, not to mention her own grandfather, and kill Tahl if didn't comply. So if Peyton had become a *situation*, so be it.

"We have no reason to doubt it," Jett said somberly. "As distasteful as it seems."

There was a moment of silence as everyone contemplated what that meant. Tahl's hand twitched against her thigh.

"So this means Desi didn't jinx your relationship with Peyton."

Jett would likely frown on his sister shaking his mate until her teeth rattled in her head, so Desi contented herself with a death glare in River's direction.

Tahl laughed. "Unless she cast a spell, I'd say that Peyton did that all by herself. It was never real."

She couldn't look at him and knew Marlene was looking anywhere else too. The weight of his hand lifted and she repressed the intense need to flee.

"Desi?" He'd turned to face her, two fingers gently lifting her chin. She forced herself to look into his eyes.

"I have an … ability, it seems." *Besides being able to shift.*

"What kind of ability?"

"If I'm upset enough with someone I tend to say things—wish them on them—and they come true."

"Okay," he drew it out. "And that affected me and Peyton how?"

"I wished you the best and that you got what you needed."

He shook his head. "You think you stuck me with Peyton?"

"No!" How thick was he? "I spoiled what you had with her."

"I had nothing with her, Desiree. She compelled me, remember? It was all false."

But she'd been nothing but resentful, aside from their … sexual interludes.

"I'd like to think I got what I needed," he added. "But did you? Or do you still feel betrayed by tradition and destiny?"

"I told you I was saving myself for someone who deserved me." His features tightened and his eyes grew blank, so she hurried to finish. "You've always been that man, Tahl, at least that was my hope. My pride got in the way. And my guilt."

"Baby." He took in a big breath. "Okay. I fucked up, triggering your heat. Not exactly conducive to building trust. But here on in you talk to me. Do you understand?"

"I do. I will." He was asking a lot, but she'd try.

A throat cleared, and she stilled. Tahl's eyes widened a fraction and she realized he'd also forgotten they weren't alone. Hot color eased up her throat to flush her cheeks. Scarlet, if the heat was any indication.

"Simon is of the opinion you influencing the outcome of events in other people's lives is unlikely." Her mother dropped the bombshell with no particular inflection in her voice.

"What?" Desi leaned forward, thwarted by Tahl's apparent need to keep his hands on her. "But you agreed with me!"

A faraway look on her face, her mother said,

"You displayed no evidence of your heritage growing up, Desiree. Jett's Fae side was apparent from birth, but he's male, and his father is an Alpha. I suppose I wanted to believe you had the ability to influence others and it lent weight to the argument."

Not for the first time, she wanted to choke her parent, and she felt River's animosity clear across the room. Her friend opened her mouth but was cut off by her mate.

"You meddle, Mom. You cause trouble." Jett's features were set in uncompromising lines and Marlene flinched.

"I tried to reassure you, Desi, especially when you told me about your visions. I'd talked with Simon, you see."

"Visions?" Tahl beat everyone else to it. "You have visions?"

"Just one. I had it twice." She glared at her mother. "I've been a mess, thinking I'd…"

"Well, you still would have thought Tahl chose you second. Better you think you had some control over the situation."

Furious, she blinked and then swallowed to avoid unloading on dear old mom. She loved Marlene, but it was hard to like the woman sometimes. Tahl was still muttering about visions.

"I saw myself standing over you with blood on my hands," she told him. "Okay? And there might have been a moment where I wondered if I'd… Well, you know."

"You *were* pissed off," he concurred.

"Not that pissed off."

"And it came true? The vision?"

"She packed your wounds, Tahl. It was like being in stasis, immobilized after Peyton compelled me, but I could see and hear everything as it played out. Desi's hands were covered in your blood." Jett drew everyone's attention before they looked back at her.

Unable to bear the stares of shock and horror, she dropped her gaze. Tahl wrapped her up, his warm breath against her temple, as he asked, "What happened, Jett?"

"Peyton planned to kill us all, including you if you wouldn't join her. Consort, I think she called you. Desiree shifted to stop her. Broke her spine. It was fucking amazing."

Amazing? Her brother had looked anything but amazed when he'd left them the night before. Shocked, horrified, stunned, maybe. But amazed?

"I'd say that's her true Fae heritage, Marlene," Simon said.

"I don't want to be different," Desiree said, her voice small in the big space. Simon's little lecture hadn't been lost on her.

"It's a big responsibility," Simon agreed. "And one that appears to be brought about under extreme duress—and protectiveness. Hopefully, you'll never find yourself in such a situation again. But I'd think it was worth it in this case."

It was hard to disagree with him, this old Fae. She wondered if there were other things that went bump in the night and resolved to ask him what he knew.

"The only people aware you can shift are contained in this room."

"But, Alpha Leaf—"

"Didn't see your wolf. Only the aftermath, and he's not inclined to question it too closely. You somehow got the jump on the threat. Period. She wasn't dead, but thoroughly incapacitated." Her brother paused. "This won't go before the Council."

Jett's leadership was such that the final word had

been spoken, and she let herself relax a little.

River took Marlene into the kitchen, ostensibly to make some food and coffee, while Jett asked Simon to accompany him to his office. Desi suspected her brother meant to garner as much information as possible from the man, rather than rely on their mother. It wasn't really Marlene's fault. She'd been orphaned at a young age, growing up in foster homes before meeting Jett's father, and she had her own, strong ideas. Ones that didn't necessarily mean obeying her son, even if he was Alpha.

The union with River's old Alpha was still shrouded in mystery, at least for her and Lizbeth, born long after Jett and to a different male, and while they knew their mother wasn't human—or shifter—she knew as little about her Fae heritage as they did. Desi stared after Simon, hoping to pick his brain.

"Jett has to do what's right for the whole pack, baby. He'll need to know things you won't have an interest in. But I'll see to it that you and Simon have some time together."

"That's important to me."

"I know." He hugged her close.

"What's your take on me shifting?"

"Besides saving my ass?"

She wrinkled her nose. "Having a mate who can shift has to be weird."

"You concern yourself with the damnedest things, woman." He looked at her, gaze steady and open. "I'm shifter. I can shift. Seems only fair you can too. I love you, Desi. In any shape. Any form. Any mood."

She melted, trusting in him. "I can be a bitch sometimes. Difficult."

"Part of your appeal, although I can do without those figurative stabs through my heart."

"I love you, Tahl." Okay, she'd already told him

he had her heart, but saying those words made her breathless.

"Sweetest thing you've ever said." He set his mouth over hers and kissed her, a slow tasting that built until he was devouring her, savoring her very essence as she surrendered.

As they both replenished their supply of oxygen, he rested his forehead against hers. "Still want that party?"

"I do."

"I want you." He ground his erection against her pelvis.

"You have me."

He growled at her tease, and she gave into the imp of mischief riding her. Dipping around his tall body, she flew out of the room, running up the stairs with long, lithe strides. She gloried in the lightness, her burdens released and shared.

Tahl caught her outside one of the bedrooms, whirling her into the space, the door swinging shut behind them. "Running from my wolf again, baby?"

The fact that they were in her brother's house should have deterred her, but she found she didn't care. "You caught me. Again."

Shoving a hand through her hair, he tugged her close, taking charge, and her wolf rebelled. Perhaps it was riding the victory, but for once Desiree and her animal were of the same mind. She folded to her knees, her fingers efficiently dealing with her mate's fly.

His engorged cock pressed through the opening, encased in the fabric of his boxers. She dealt with them too and admired the long, thick shaft, crowned with such a wide head as she grasped him. Silk over steel.

"Jesus, Desi." His fingers clenched in her hair, the slight sting arousing her, pushing her on.

Leaning forward, she tentatively ran the flat of her tongue over the corona, savoring the tang of his seed. Tahl gave a sharp intake of breath, and his thighs tightened. Recalling how he'd explored every inch of her with his tongue, she went on her own survey, tasting and licking, nuzzling and nibbling.

When he was shifting in place, clearly unable to maintain much control, she set her mouth over him and took as much of his cock as she could, feeling him in the back of her throat. Remembering his leisurely strokes when he fucked her, she mimicked the motion, drawing back and then dipping ever deeper as she took him.

"I'm gonna come, baby." He fumbled at her hair, ineffectually tugging her away.

Her jaw aching, she sucked hard as she retreated and was rewarded with a hot, salty surge of his seed, spurting over her tongue. She swallowed frantically and released him, his sated cock still hard, glistening wet. Giving it a little pat, she glanced up at him—and froze.

His wolf stared back and hers rose to greet him. She didn't feel the least subservient, reveling in her power. Gradually, his subsided, his chiseled lips lifting into a beatific smile. "That was indescribable. Feel free to have your way with me whenever the urge strikes."

He tucked himself away and offered a hand, tugging her to her feet, pressing a kiss on her mouth. She closed her eyes the better to savor the moment.

"I think we'd better join the others."

She checked herself in the mirror. Flushed face, swollen lips, and sex hair. Tahl looked ... relaxed, but otherwise normal. Great. But did she really care if everyone knew what they'd been doing? When they knew her secret? It hardly seemed to signify. "I'm starved. Eating for two. Or three."

He went on point, blinking at her. "What?"

"Made you look."

He chuckled. "You never disappoint, baby."

Epilogue

Twins didn't run in either of their families, so maybe she shouldn't have teased Tahl about carrying more than one pup. The ultrasound had confirmed the doctor's speculation and her mate's joy had been tinged with speculation until she reminded him she didn't keep secrets anymore. Unless she was keeping one from herself.

She loved the boys, little Dominic and Duncan, but she desperately wanted some time away from the house and alone time with her mate. The man in question strode in, wearing a pair of broken-in jeans and a soft, button-down shirt. He'd rolled the cuffs back to display his impressively muscled forearms, and while she appreciated the show, her gaze drifted lower, to those jeans.

"Desi!" Tahl's mouth dropped open, a look he could pull off given his handsome face. "What are you wearing?"

"This little outfit?" She minced toward him, taking care to twitch her hips and make the little pink skirt flare. The more pronounced curve of her hips caused the garment to ride up her thighs even higher, and she somehow smothered a smile when her mate's eyes flared.

Her breasts, larger with the advent of the babies, were barely contained by the blouse, and she knew her new, lacy, pink bra showed seductively behind the white fabric. The effect of her movements was slightly challenged by the pink thongs slapping over the floor, but he could give her points for trying.

"Fuck," he groaned, passing a big hand over his fly. "Jeans suck when you've got a hard on."

"I take it you like it, then?" She posed, fingertips sifting through her hair.

"You'd look good in a paper bag. Maybe we should stay in."

"No way, buddy. We're going to have dinner someplace where baby food isn't on the menu, and dancing afterward is. Nothing fancy, not dressed like this."

"I can't believe you kept that outfit, baby."

"First thing you ever gave me? Besides your cock? Of course, I kept it."

He choked and then laughed, before crossing to his dresser. Carefully removing the contents of the middle drawer, laying them on top, he lifted the paper lining the bottom. Plastic crinkled. "I kept these. Interesting you took two tests."

"You kept my pee sticks?" She felt her eyebrows trying to climb up past her hairline. "Eew."

"They're in a baggie."

"Still." She tried to tease him past the moisture blurring her vision.

"Don't, baby. I can't deal when you cry. Don't." He tossed the sticks on the dresser and rushed her. She sniffled into this shoulder, hoping she hadn't ruined her makeup.

The doorbell chimed, and she felt how torn he was. Stay and soothe? See who was at the door? "Go. I'm fine."

She put the little baggie back where he'd secreted it, and carefully layered the clothes on top, easing the drawer shut. When she made her way to the living room, Cassie had her coat off and Tahl was finding her a hanger.

"Hi, Cass. I can't tell you how appreciative I am that you'll watch the boys tonight."

Cassie gave her a sweet smile that didn't hide her drawn features or the shadows beneath her dark eyes. "I'm happy to do it. With the kids away with River and Jett, that house is far too big for me."

"You're not alone in it, are you?" Tahl immediately reacted. "You can stay here."

Desi hid her wince. They were about to start the addition on their current house, adding two more bedrooms in anticipation of a least one more child. To say things were a little crowded with twins was an understatement, her office now a nursery and the living room inundated with kid *stuff*. Cassie would have to sleep on a blow-up mattress.

"I'm not alone, Tahl. Jett would never allow that. Benjamin is in charge."

There was a wealth of implication in those four words and Desi scrambled to decipher a few of them. Tahl's eyes narrowed as he focused on Cassie. "Are you okay?"

"Me? Sure, I'm fine. Just a little tired is all. But not too tired to be careful with Duncan and Dominic!"

"I'm not worried," she reassured the young female. "They're sleeping right now and might stay that way until we get home. If not, there's breast milk in the fridge to heat and some food. I labeled them."

"Everything is labeled, Cassie. Everything. And readily available." Tahl's fond smile took the sting out of his comment. Who knew she'd become OCD after delivering their children? It was the only way she could stay on top of mothering, working and, let's not forget, sating an extremely randy male shifter.

"It'll be nice to not have to worry." Cassie looked around, and patently ignored the pinging of her cell.

"Want to get that?" Tahl was anal about answering phones, viewing them as a possible lifeline.

"I'm good. I know who it is. I'll call back later."

Looking askance, he nodded and searched through the closet for her coat. "I'm taking Desi to Georgie's. She has a craving for diner food and they have a jukebox."

Cassie looked between them and laughed. "Have a good time. I'll call if anything happens, I promise. And I'll answer your calls."

Rushing back to check on her sleeping babies, she patted the little, upturned bottoms and leaned in to press a kiss on each tiny forehead. Tahl laid a hand on her ass, and she squeaked, again wondering how he could move so silently. Together, they stared at the little creatures they'd made, smiling as Dominic pursed his tiny mouth and hitched higher. Duncan twitched as if in response to his younger brother.

"We could stay home. Order in. Dance in the living room. Cassie can run interference with the little guys." Tahl worked an arm around her and tucked her up against his side. His scent comforted her and she pressed closer.

"We'd probably shock that little shifter, and I suspect she needs some time by herself."

"Then let's go, before I remove that little skirt, and find out what you're wearing beneath it."

"Anticipation is good for you," she teased, before slipping from his grasp and hurrying to the foyer.

Watching him stalk toward her, his gait somewhat impaired by an obvious bulge below his waistband, she took a moment to appreciate her good luck. Tahl's expression changed from that of lust and possession to tenderness, love shining in those gem-like eyes.

Taking her arm, he escorted her to their respectable SUV, the Camaro and her sports car garaged in deference to the additions to the family. He handed her in, leaning to steal a kiss that she willingly gave.

They'd both been undone by destiny, and in the best possible way.

The End

www.allysonyoung.com

ALLYSON YOUNG

EVERNIGHT PUBLISHING ®

www.evernightpublishing.com